DOLORES and MILAGROS

a story for our innocence

narrated by

María Benedetti

DOLORES and MILAGROS
a story for our innocence

English version of *Dolores y Milagros: una historia para la inocencia*

Translation by the author.

ISBN: 978-0-9633440-6-9

© María Benedetti (María Dolores Hajosy Benedetti) 2018
   www.botanicultura.com
   botanicultura@gmail.com

Cover art: Saraivy Orench Reinat
   www.facebook.com/saraivy.orenchreinat
   saraivy@hotmail.com

Cover design:
   Carmen R. Lebrón Anaya
   www.facebook.com/crladesign
   lebronanaya@gmail.com

This micronovel is a production of BURENKEN,
with a branch in nearly everybody's neighborhood.

I dedicate this story to the people I have interviewed . . .
and to the protagonists that live within us.

---

birth of
Geña (1898) in barrio Almácigo
Abelarda (1926) in barrio Piñales
Mago (1953) in barrio Piñales
Lola (1955) in New York City
Valeria (1964) in barrio Piñales

Gratitude

for those who inspired this novel
and the stories that are woven within it,
with humble acknowledgement of our shared destiny
and of my responsibility to tell this tale
with integrity and grace.
I hope to have been a worthy reporter.

for my brave, patient and honest readers for
critiquing, suggesting, understanding and challenging me:
Carla Cavina, Joel Franqui, Eliván Martínez,
Francisca "Paca" Díaz Díaz, Laura Cotte Emannueli,
Emilio Rodríguez, Érica Martínez Atabei,
Sergio Yoel Bermúdez, Abadha Lila Cintrón,
Giles André Smith, Evelyn Díaz Cruz,
Vanessa Raquel Arjona, Sheyda Gómez.

for the trees, our paper.
for the trees, our shelter.
for the trees, nourishment.
for the trees, medicine.
for the trees, clean air, shade and fresh green coolness.
for the trees, tables and pencils, beds and boxes,
floors and nests, walls and plates.
for the trees, colors, toys, perfume,
wind breaks, rope, hideouts, guitars.
for the trees, skyscrapers and community life
under the forest floor,
beauty and peace.
for the trees, our drums.
for the trees, our friends.

Contents

Prologue

Personal notes

•

Traumatized by an earthquake, a tidal wave and hurricane San Felipe, my maternal family left Mayagüez, Puerto Rico toward the end of the 1920s and never returned. Sixty years later, I came back: daughter of María del Perpetuo Socorro, granddaughter of María Cristina y Carmelo María. I came as yet another María, cultural journalist and student of the botanical medicine of my northern, New York region.

Inspired by exciting classes in Puerto Rican culure, folklore, history and literature with José Manuel Torres Santiago and other great professors at Hunter College, my goal was to learn about and document the tradition of Borinquen's botanical folk medicine through interviews with mothers and grandmothers, bone setters, barefoot doctors, midwives, farmers and other wise people experienced in the use of the archipelago's medicinal plants.

During that first visit, I discovered linguistic, spiritual and other cultural jewels as well as great practical wisdom. The elders I interviewed moved my soul with the depth of their love for other human beings and for the plants that surrounded them. Their botanical knowledge was impressive. The relevance and effectiveness of their healing practices amazed and inspired me, and I was alarmed by the possibility that these might disappear. So much so that I decided to abandon my life in New York and move to the island as

a way of anchoring my commitment. Without a clue,
I ended up moving to the very same *barrio* where my
maternal grandmother had married and began raising
her children. I soon got a job as an environmental
journalist with the University of Puerto Rico in
Mayagüez, where I continued my studies of Puerto
Rican culture, literature and history. And I kept on
with my interviews, including over two dozen artisanal
fishermen and women from Cabo Rojo to Vieques.

   The wisdom grew and reproduced. The amazing
images and memories that I tape-recorded transformed
me and asked for a public forum. The elders' stories
started to wake me at night, whispering insistently.
My professional publications excluded hundreds of
tales, images and perspectives belonging to a vibrant
but invisibilized agricultural/fisheries culture. I now
present some of these tales, images and perspectives
among *dolores* and *milagros*, sorrows and miracles,
hopeful that they will find an honorable place here.
May you enjoy meeting the fictionalized *abuelos* whose
intense love and vast knowledge changed my own
life. These people, so intensely identified with nature,
practiced a broad, syncretizedand spirituality that
defies classification and inspired in me great respect.

   Until the middle of the 20th century, the agro-
ecological culture of Borinquen was a repository of vast
knowledge that allowed and will continue to allow for
human survival based upon our renewable resources.
For many reasons, this body of knowledge was – both

deliberately and unconsciously – associated with
backwardness, poverty, ignorance and "undesireable"
racial profiles. So within these pages I've enjoyed
celebrating this knowledge. I also proudly affirm our
unique way of expressing Boricua Spanish with so
many roots in the Taino, African, European and Jíbaro
experience. So the Spanish edition of this book is filled
with uniformity-defying words only spoken in Puerto
Rico and which – with every utterance – strengthen our
feelings of nationality and cultural belonging. (This
book's extensive glossary invites English-language
readers to participate in the fun.)

With the love and respect that I have for our
elders, the ecosystems of our archipelago and our
"escape-to-make-our-own-culture" traditions of
freedom, I present this text as a way of sharing scenes
inspired by the humble people that have never stopped
whispering to me. I hope that in the fiction inspired by
their words (and by our losses) we come together and get
closer to a history that was broadly shared, remembered
. . . and later prohibited.

I dared to weave in stories based on my own
experiences and those of friends and neighbors, but I
warn you that this book is pure fiction, written only to
evoke. There is nothing to believe. Just feel, visualize,
savor, remember, imagine.

May this book offer another story of another
Borikén, inherited, created and re-created in our
unique and miraculous way for our collective wellbeing,

our senses of humor and justice, for our children and grandchildren . . . and for our sacred innocence.

And may you, my honorable readers, enjoy the flavor or my humble experiment, cooked over a low flame for you with love and sincere devotion.

María Benedetti

The story

(You get to make the connections.)

Chapter one

Born standing

•

Up in the *corazón* tree, Abelarda felt the first
piercing, rhythmic pains. That day, her sixth baby would
arrive, so she was hurrying to harvest all the fruit she
could carry.

Since dawn, an unmistakable aroma, like sweet
cream with spices, had called to her: sun-warmed
corazones on the hilly terrain of Piñales, her *barrio.*
Driven by the urgency of her ninth-month cravings, she
didn't even stop to milk the goat. She left the house
running, as well as she could, up the hill just as soon as
she'd served a breakfast of coffee and hearth-roasted
sweet potatoes to her husband Calixto and the little
ones, who left early for the farm with aunty Rafaela.

Traipsing up the hill, Abelarda glanced at the
mare, and laughed remembering how they'd all criticized
her for riding "like a man" – and not sitting sideways,
with her legs demurely closed – until the first weeks
of her seventh month. Smiling, she walking on with
the rhythm of a woman on a mission: a secret escape
from interminable domestic labors despite an imminent
childbirth.

•

It wasn't easy with so much belly, but she climbed
up the tree little by little, feeling how the living wood
crunched as it gave under her weight.

"Now you're in trouble," she murmured, struggling to breathe as she pushed past the tree's fourth major branch. There, the *corazón* tree's limbs squeezed her like never before, barely allowing her to grasp a dozen ripe fruits with the hand-woven net bag that hung from her bamboo pole. She stretched her aching arms as she coached herself: "Little by little! Little by little!" Covered with sweat, she carefully guided the pole so the fruits would fall gently onto the earth. "Hard to believe that no one else has noticed this. All these *corazones* ripe at one time . . . and still on the tree! Perfect for me! I'll take all I can get for folks to eat after I push out this baby."

Eight stretches and five *corazones* later, she felt a sharp pain that took away her strength but not the desire to finish what she had started. "No, no! I've come this far. I'm not gonna leave those *corazones* hanging on the tree!"

Just when she started to relax, another sweaty wave of acute pain left her legs like *tembleque de coco*. Resigned, she looked longingly at the branch that awaited her a bit higher on the tree and suddenly felt water running down her legs. "¡*Caramba!* My water broke and look where I am hanging!", she said out loud to calm herself as she shivered. The idea of giving birth so far off the ground humbled her enough to ask for help from the very tree that she had saved as a child after a hail storm. "Help me! Help me, *corazón*, like I helped you," she begged as she lowered herself through air and tree limbs, until she could finally feel the *barrio's* holy ground beneath her feet.

She rested a bit among the *corazones*. As soon as
she could, she placed the fragrant fruits inside an agave-
fiber sack, which she gently slung over her shoulder.
Then she walked with her still-shaky legs down the hill
toward her home.

From the trail, she could hear the noisy chatter
of young women on their way down to the river to wash
their families' clothing. "Cesi! Cesi!", called Abelarda, as
she approached her home. "Tell Tomasa to come right
away. My water broke!"

Cecilia Méndez Vargas, a fourteen-year old with
wheat-colored skin, incisive dark eyes and a wild head of
hair gave a frightened look to her voluminous neighbor.

"Tomasa is in Cuyón with *doña* Margarita. She left
last night in a hurry on Mister Rovira's mare."

"OK, well then *you'll* have to help me out. You can
do it! Come!"

"Me?"

"Of course, my love. You're her apprentice, and
today it's your turn to catch a baby. Come on. It will be
easy. I've already been through this five times so I'll tell
you what to do. Listen to me now. I'm going to light the
fire. Bring the moonshine and Moncho's knife. But don't
be long. Get going!"

Cecilia felt her face burning and her stomach
turning as she ran to get the tools of what would soon
be her profession. Not that she wanted to be a midwife!

No way! But Tomasa had adopted her when her parents died of typhoid fever two years before. She was left alone in the world when her brothers went to work with uncle Carmelo in the city.

"Learn to be a good midwife, *mi hija*," he had counseled gently. "It's a respectable profession and everyone will treat you like family."

Cecilia tearfully accepted her destiny. She knew her uncle was right. Besides, there was no place for her in the old man's hut, and she owed her cooperation to Tomasa, who treated her well, although impatiently at times.

To be fair, it should go on record that Cecilia Méndez Vargas had *not* been born to aid women in childbirth. She much preferred the idea of going to the city, cleaning rich people's houses and seeing the world. It was out of pure loyalty that she ran to don Moncho's place for the neighborhood's best blade and a bottle of homemade rum.

•

Grateful to have arrived, Abelarda left the sack of *corazones* at the entrance of her home and walked heavily toward the wood-burning *fogón*. On the way, she asked a low-growing avocado tree for five new leaves for her birthing brew. Then she revived her cooking fire with a smoldering stick of *almácigo* wood. She left the saucepan with spring water over the flame and breathed long and slow. Then she heated up the irons that would warm her poultice wraps. When she saw the water ready to boil, she cut up the avocado leaves with a prayer and placed them amongst the bubbles. She left her tea simmering while she went out to harvest – with the greatest of respect – three, large *palma christi* leaves that would support her labor and alleviate the pain. She softened them with the steam of her tea, and then rubbed them with oil she had extracted from the seeds of another *palma christi* plant a few weeks earlier. Somehow, between contractions, she managed to iron her first round of clean, thick flannel wraps and walked slowly with them and her green allies to the mattress stuffed with balsa fibers on the floor.

She crouched down to lay on her bed bordering the wall. There, she covered her belly with the big, oily leaves, and placed the warm wraps on top. Finally, she could surrender to simply feeling the painful pressures that moved from the volcano of her womb. Her baby was coming. Her baby was on his way.

She tried to be still. Two minutes. Three. When Cecilia came running in with a bottle of transparent liquid, a tin of coconut oil, a keenly sharpened knife and clean blankets to receive the baby, Abelarda was sitting up, leaning against the wall. Leaves and warm flannel covered her ready belly.

"Honey, bring me my avocado-leaf tea. I'm not moving another inch!"

Obedient, Cecilia found the decoction that would provoke a quick and easy labor. She served it with molasses, which would give her neighbor extra strength for what was to come. Then she ironed more flannel and easily slid the warm rags over the oil-softened leaves. So far, all was well, and the midwife's apprentice began to feel comfortable.

"Come on, girl. It's time for my belly rub. This baby's coming," suggested Abelarda after savoring the semi-bitter sweetness at the bottom of her cup.

The moment Cecilia so dreaded had finally arrived. "Ok," she uttered in a nervous whisper. "I'll just wash my hands here." And with a splash of moonshine, she rubbed her hands with exaggerated cleanliness, trying to organize her thoughts. She did not remember the midwife's prayer, nor did she bow her head before the carved image of the Mother of Miracles, *la Milagrosa*, on the wall. She gave a quick, uncertain look toward the mess of sheets and rags, towels and blankets. Then, without looking at Abelarda, Cecilia for the first time did what she had observed Tomasa do on ever-so-many occasions. She drank a goodly ration of the burning alcohol directly from the bottle.

"*¡Carájila!*", she spit, as half of her mouthful jettisoned toward Abelarda, who moaned as she held her well-covered womb. Then the little midwife sat up and, somewhat calmer, slid her hands beneath the soft leaves and flannel in order to massage her neighbor's belly. Less than ten seconds had passed when her innocent hands froze. "The baby's not coming right. The baby's coming foot first, Abelarda! It's a footling!"

"Massage me hard, girl. My baby is coming just fine!", begged the belabored.

Then Abelarda gave an uncontrolled birthing shriek. "Ok, baby. You're coming now. Uuuuuh. It's *now*!" Abelarda moved away from the wall so she could kneel above the towels and blankets and wait for the push that would bring her sixth child into the light.

"But it's feet first, Abelarda. The baby can't be born like that!"

"It's being born alright. This baby's on its way. You'll have to pull."

Abelarda pushed with a long grunt. The pain was worse than what she had felt during other births.

At that moment, the wall boards of palm wood began to spin around Cecilia's head. "I'm gonna get *doña* Leonor!", she yelled as she ran out the door, her face wet with tears burning of alcohol, terror and shame.

"Don't leave me, Ceci!", begged Abelarda, as she watched a stream of scarlet flow from her innards. "Don't abandon me now!"

The situation was serious and she was alone. The receiving blankets were turning red before her eyes.

Abelarda did not have to look at the carved image to remember the one who'd always accompanied her and her family. Their devotion had filled her home with a golden glow that emanated from the ever-burning flame before a figure carved in aromatic cedar wood.

"*Milagrosa*, Mother of Miracles, I surrender to you and I surrender the life of my baby to your infinite care, your tender goodness. Help me now as you always have. Hail Mary, full of grace, Mother of God. Intercede for me, *María de los Milagros*." Then, Abelarda fit her entire right hand into the jar of aromatic coconut oil and asked: "May my hand be blessed, may my hand be yours, *Milagrosa*, Mother God." And with her most extreme effort, she bent over to try and fish out her baby.

Just a little closer. Come on, now. Just a bit more. She felt a tiny foot. "Come, my baby! Mother of Life, help me now. Bring this baby down!"

She pushed again and felt her womb opening with a burning hot pain accompanied by another bath of blood. She pushed one more time, and then, weakened, she managed only to lean one shoulder on the rustic wooden wall and stay on her knees above the blankets.

Then, among the impatient calls of a she-goat and the proud song of the yard's biggest rooster, Abelarda felt a light movement – a caress of silk – right above her head, and a whisper of courage without words.

She pushed with a long scream and another wave of pain. Overwhelmed with vertigo she cried out: "I can't lie down, *Milagrosa*. ¡Push for me now!"

She stretched again toward the baby between her legs and discovered that now she could feel both feet. Encouraged, she pulled softly, enduring an incomparable sensation of being invaded and being emptied all at once until – with one last scream and a visceral convulsion –

the baby slid down her canal and touched, feet first, the bloody blankets awaiting him. Heartened, Abelarda managed to grab him and bring him to her chest.

Finally, she allowed herself to fall back into bed with the bloody baby in her arms, as she prayed to her protector, now to give thanks and name her boy: Manuel. Manuel Milagros. "Manuel Milagros, you were born standing," she whispered with the last fiber of her voice, satisfied that her baby was sucking hard, while the umbilical cord kept pulsing.

After Abelarda had pushed out her placenta and recovered from that last spasm, Cecilia ran in with *abuela* Leonor, who had already drunk a full glass of courage.

Cecilia – filled with admiration for the bravery of her neighbor – ran straight to the back yard. There, amidst tears that only added to her confusion, she took the initiative of digging out and cutting a big piece of the base of a banana plant. Quickly she took it inside to grate it and squeeze out the juice that would staunch Abelarda's hemorrhage. Then she put three long branches of rosemary herb in a dry, iron pan on the hearth.

Leonor gathered blankets and sacks for raising Abelarda's hips. When the umbilical cord was finally still, she tied and cut it. With encouraging words, she began to press the belly points that would help to stop the flow of blood.

Cecilia coaxed Abelarda to drink the banana sap from a dark spoon carved from coconut shell. After bathing the baby, the little midwife prepared a paste of rosemary ash with copaiba oil, *aceite de palo*, to disinfect and cure his belly button. Then she covered it with a shiny, new penny, donated by Moncho, the baby's godfather, and she bandaged the copper-covered knot with a long swatch of clean, white fabric. This treatment would protect the baby from fungus, infection and more. Finally, she walked toward the tobacco ranch to bury what was left of the umbilical cord and placenta in the place most appropriate for a boy who was destined to be a farmer.

For the first time, Cecilia had gone beyond the stage of just observing and doing errands. In spite of having abandoned Abelarda at the most critical moment of her labor, Cecilia was filled with a sense of purpose and respect for the profession she had always rejected. By the time she had milked the goat and prepared a restorative pigeon broth, she felt slightly transformed. The words midwife and even "baby catcher" suddenly sounded like courage and blessed wisdom shared among the women – grandmothers and young ones – of her community.

•

Little by little, relatives and neighbors began to arrive, alarmed by the news that, after a rest of nearly seven years, Abelarda's sixth baby was coming out feet first. A footling! Dangerous indeed.

By the time Calixto and his brother Daniel arrived panting from the farm, Abelarda, exhausted, could only say: "Manuel Milagros." She smiled, proud of her birthing, and of a son who had come into this world with so much divine protection.

Calixto fell to his knees to kiss his wife on the forehead and to inspect all the details of his new baby boy. Cecilia hurried off to milk the family's goat.

Among prayers and riddles, the neighbors enjoyed their time in Abelarda's home. There were *corazones* and *café con leche* for all, and a sensation of well being extended to them from a golden light before the *Madre Milagrosa*, portal of life, of death, of miracles. *La Milagrosa*, mother of all that exists, reined there that day, innocently dressed as a virgin, carved in aromatic cedar wood with sincere devotion and infinite wisdom.

Chapter two

Osaín's goat

•

Born thanks to divine intervention, Manuel
Milagros, known as Mago, had additional protections.
His aunt Rafaela, an active *espiritista*, recognized in
her favorite nephew a need for the knowledge of certain
disciplines, especially those that would help him avoid
being hurt by envious souls or the wandering dead.

"Innocence is protection for little children, but
you're growing up now and you'll be needing some skills,
my love. Remember what I'm about to tell you, and
you'll avoid all kinds of disasters." Rafaela had tried
to share her message many times, but the boy resented
the words of precaution that changed the color of his
world. Until one steamy afternoon in May, the shocking
news of Maelo Posada's mysterious death reached them
as he and his aunt shelled white beans, surrounded by
the sweet and soothing aroma of ylang ylang flowers.
That day, when Rafaela told him what he would have to
do in order to protect himself from threatening forces,
the well-meaning words of his aunt were a balsam to his
soul.

•

Summertimes, when the boys of Piñales finished
their farm chores, they would gather at Charco Prieto,
their hideout among the rocks and waterfalls of the
river. There, they dove from boulders into the water and
conspired to supplement their everyday diet of boiled

viandas, homemade cheese, greens with hot pepper, and coffee with goat's milk. Some days, the *charco* smelled like fruit: guavas, mangos, *guanábanas* or *guamá.* Other days, there were fresh water crabs or tiny prawns or a pair of birds mysteriously missing from doña Cecilia's pigeon coop. The group of seven to thirteen boys obeyed a strict code of honor. If any one of them found something to eat, all would share the bounty.

In a cave bordering the charco, the boys stored – for preparing their stews – dry firewood and a five-gallon pot that Wiso had rescued from Hacienda La Torre after the fire. The cave also boasted a seashell trumpet prepared by Toño, two long wooden spoons carved by Dino, and a full set of calabash and coconut shell tableware made by the entire tribe, since stealing utensils from their homes would have earned them physical discipline from mothers strengthened by undending agro-domestic labors. There was also a jar of salt to condiment the soups they made with sweet and hot peppers, rosemary, wild *culantro,* two varieties of oregano leaves and all the *viandas* and edible wild greens they could get their hands on.

•

One day, before stopping by the *charco*, Mago went to inspect the *guanábana* trees at the good *santero* Joaquín Pinares' farm. He was eager to see if he'd be lucky enough to gather some of the fruit that was ripening there. But something far more interesting hung from one of those trees. A freshly-killed young goat hung from a low branch. To Mago, that was a lottery-level, grand prize! His mouth was already watering! Having just turned twelve, a month after Maelo Posada's strange death, Mago breathed deeply. Then, remembering his aunty Rafaela and the recently deceased, he urinated before cautiously extending his left hand to touch that goat.

The animal sacrificed to Osaín, the *orisha* of the forest, was obviously a favor bestowed upon him from the Divine. So the best way to give thanks would be ... to eat it! The only hitch was that Mago would have to lie to his friends, whose respectful fear of the Cuban and his rites would veto their enjoyment of such a feast.

As he untied the animal, he felt its weight. It was a small, 40-pound goat. Its meat would be tender and oh-so delicious.

Just as Manuel Milagros eased the goat over his shoulder, he heard the Cuban's voice as he walked downhill from his home toward the orchard. He was conversing with his friend, a priest of the ancient Afro-Caribbean religion.

With no time to waste, the youth took off running with his treasure through the trails he knew far better than the farm's middle-aged owner. It wasn't easy. The animal was heavy and the boy nearly slid all the way down the rustic pathways of rocks and red clay. He left a stony lane of blood as he got away from the angry cries of Joaquín, whose honor depended upon his presention of that goat to his congregation in just a few hours.

Manuel Milagros was soaked in blood. He had not stopped to consider the possible consequences of having stolen from a delegate of the African gods. His mind was fully occupied thinking about how he would convince his pals that the goat had been a gift.

Meanwhile, the indignant Joaquín Pinares followed the red trail, shooting upward with his rifle until he understood that the thief's agility far surpassed his own. "For Gods' sake!", he shouted finally, before turning toward the scene of the crime, where his companion, a *babalao*, squatted to throw the coconut shells and thus investigate the meaning of the robbery of Osaín's goat.

"Eje ife," pronounced the babalao. "Before the eyes of Ifá, the thief is . . . innocent!", he declared just as Mago reached the river's edge with his prize. The solitary word pronounced by the priest calmed Joaquín's fury, because although he didn't like the idea, he had to accept that for some reason, Osaín – the goat's true owner – had in no way been offended by the theft.

•

So as not to frighten the others with the bloody mess he'd made of his clothing, Mago took off his shirt when he got to the river. As he rubbed it clean under a *pomarrosa* tree, hard-earned copper pennies fell from his pocket into the water. Finally, he squatted to bathe himself with leaves and golden river sand as he prepared the speech that would allow a banquet to proceed.

He got to the *charco* early. Only Dino was present among the boulders in the river, breaking thick, tropical carob pods with the clan's Taíno hatchet, made of a perfectly-formed, large black stone, exquisitely polished by the river.

"Dino! Dinín!", called Mago between heavy breaths. "You are not going to believe this! Pinares gave us guys this goat!"

At fourteen, Dino was the eldest of the group and the son of Moncho the pig farmer. He not only had access to the best knives in the neighborhood; he had *lots* of experience skinning animals of all sizes.

"You lie! The whole goat?", he asked incredulous.

"I swear to God! He said it was a gift because he had to kill two today, and one was going to be left over, and that nothing could be left over because that would be a sin."

Mago had gently placed their goat in the shade and now gesticulated with his arms as if to convince himself of the story. The "sin" part did not sound like Joaquín, who *never* mentioned the "s" word. So he quickly added his most convincing argument. "The only thing he wants from us is that we give him back the hide. He's gonna need it to make some drums."

When he saw that Dino had swallowed the tale, he finished his flamboyant presentation with a proposal: "How about we make a giant stew?"

Dino's face lit up with joy and pride, since he was the best prepared to carry out the biggest job. "I'll be right back with Pai's knives. Call everyone else and tell them to bring oranges and wine and everything they can find for our stew. I'll be right back."

Dino went to get his tools. Mago called to the group with their *fotuto*, a foot-long, seashell trumpet, and waited for the others to arrive.

They were all thrilled to find that instead of the same old salty prawn broth or the same insipid mixture of watery fruit, they would soon be eating a delicious, filling and energizing banquet of fresh goat. With boundless joy, each one went off to find whatever he could offer from his home: an onion, an orange, collard greens, a ripe breadfruit, a handful of cherry tomatoes, whole branches of oregano and *recao*, matches, another large pot for the bunch of green bananas that Wiso would beg from Mr. Bizco, and even a bottle of wine (El Pavo brand) for the stew. Later, each one would put his own special talents to work. And so it was: Toño and Nesto gathered kindling and dry logs of all sizes from the cave and from the forest. Then they got the fire going while Dino and Grabiel skinned the goat with great care, conscious that his hide would be used to make the sacred drums of their generous neighbor. Filo, Beto, Cheo and Mago cut up the meat, separating and wrapping in breadfruit leaves an ample piece for each boy's family. Then they went to work preparing the stew. A bit later, while Dino played his bongo drum,

Wiso improvised off-color verses about Minerva, their neighbor, the greatness of Joaquín Pinares and the life and doings of the goat that would soon be devoured. Mago lay back, enjoying the whirlwind of activity his deed had generated and the tantalizing aroma of a once-in-a-lifetime meal.

If the boys had stopped to look, they might have seen an ancient, one-eyed, embodied African spirit sitting in the flowering *pomarrosa* tree. That was Osaín, *orisha* of the forest, of the wild places. He was the spirit of the nutritious wild fruits, roots and weeds that had sustained so many escaped slaves and their clandestine communities. Osaín observed his happy clan of nine hard-working boys with delight. He was deeply honored to see the zeal with which they brought everything they could find from the gardens, farms and homes of Piñales to make a feast out of an animal sacrificed to Him.

Besides the great pleasure that Osaín felt seeing so much youthful energy whirling around his little goat, the spirit of the forest was doubly satisfied! That morning, Joaquín Pinares was obliged to sacrifice yet another animal for his hungry congregation. Osaín would only have to get the goat skins to Joaquín in the most conciliatory and joyful circumstances. An easy job for a divinity of the ancient Yoruba tradition!

Finally, deeply moved himself, Manuel Milagros confessed to his cohorts that he had actually robbed the goat, with his left hand, just in case. But by that time, any fear they might have felt was far exceeded by the mysterious pleasure of having fed themselves from the abundance of their *barrio* and of having eaten a meal fit for the Gods. To each and every one of them, *that* tasted like big-time innocence: pure and joyful and free of all sin.

Chapter three

Lola gets discovered

•

Lola's innocence was something else altogether.

She began studying the art of massage at an
early age when her mother figured out how to enjoy
a nap without worrying about the whereabouts of her
adventuresome, four-year-old daughter. Mami discovered
that she could simply ask Lola to play her toes as if they
were piano keys. That's how she would get her much-
needed rest. According to instructions, when Lola got
tired of playing, she would leave her hands laying upon
her mother's feet and ask the baby Jesus to bestow the
best of health upon her entire family.

Lola enjoyed converting her mother's toes into a
piano that played extravagant notes that only she could
hear among gentle snores and the dearest of maternal
aromas. It was delicious to rest her hands upon her
mother's feet and visualize healing light filling their
bedroom.

When she was ten, she began working on her father,
whose ever-growing forehead troubled him greatly. Right
after dinner, Lola would rub his scalp with her coconut
oil and leather sole tonic. She rubbed with all her might.
It was greatly entertaining to invigorate her father's
"baldy bean" with her ancestral concoctions. Her dad,
with eyes closed and a contemplative smile, enjoyed his
daughter's energetic scalp scrubbings. He had shown
her the technique himself with his "brain blooming"

massages administered every Saturday in order to avoid
in his children the progressive baldness that made him
feel older every day. "One day you'll thank me for this!,"
he declared in response to the tearful screeches of her
little brother, who received special attentions for being a
boy.

Lola enjoyed those Saturday "scrubs" because she'd
discovered that they improved her memory. From the
time she was thirteen, she studied with a hard-bristle
brush at her side. When something she read was hard
to understand, a good brushing of her hair clarified
both questions and answers.

●

As a college student in New York, Lola relished
a friendship based on readings, salsa dancing,
cooking, story telling and bicycled adventures with
Rudy Gutiérrez, a beautiful Puerto Rican guy with
very platonic tastes. Rudy studied languages, music
and – thanks to an amorous connection at the Esalen
Institute in California – the art of massage. With
fraternal trust, Lola submitted to the healing practices
of her friend. It was the seventies and in no way did it
seem odd that these encounters were done in the nude.
Their manual of techniques illustrated the massagees
without any clothing or covers, facilitating a flowing
continuity of the strokes while promoting a liberal use
of massage oil.

It would be an understatement to say that her
first full body massage changed Lola's life. It was her

second year at college and she had the flu. Every joint and muscle of her body hurt and she was all stuffed up, from her country-rough heels to her heavenly crown. Rudy began the massage with gentle pulls of her hair, working the neuralgic points on her head. When he reached her neck, Lola felt a current of relief that swam all the way down to her feet. And when Rudy touched her forearms – her forearms! – she was surprised to hear the strange moan that escaped from her being.

"Go ahead. Cry, baby," coaxed her ally who, of deep release, knew so much more than his virgin friend. The tenderness in the young masseur's voice helped her to let go of even more emotion, and she cherished the feeling inspired by a male friend, whose only agenda was her total wellbeing.

While Rudy worked on one arm and then another with all of his attention and an oil fragrant of lemongrass and pachouli, her soft but insistent cry continued, now heavy with sensations of sadness that Lola did not understand, but did recognize as her own. Later, her friend offered therapeutic pressures to her back, butt, legs and finally, her feet. When he finished his massage, Lola got up little by little, astonished to discover that her flu had disappeared!

"Holy Goddess, Rudy, you cured me! This is a miracle! A true miracle! And to think there are people . . . *old people* who have lived *many years* who have *never* received a massage in their entire lives! Lola expressed her surprise and gratitude with even more

45

tears and the euphoric sensation of having experienced one of life's great secrets. Without yet having the words to express her discovery, she was finally fully conscious that the mind, the emotions and the body are one.

After that, she began her first serious studies of human anatomy and massage strokes. Through their practices, the link between Lola and Rudy deepened to make them brother and sister, in love for eternity; although in this incarnation, at least for its most daring expressions, Rudy preferred men.

•

Just a few months after having received that first miraculous massage, Lola moved to Spain. Burning to be immersed in the language that represented her connection with the people she loved the most, she had not anticipated how demanding the European courses of linguistics, literature and anthropology could possibly be. She studied so much, ate so many cheap, fried *tapas*, and moved so very little that she gained 70 pounds in just 10 months. And although during crowded street fairs and fascinating religious processions Lola received abundant anonymous strokes below her waist, her need to be touched with warmth and respect sometimes drove her to the brink. With her body so thickened, her mind so overcharged with literary passions and her emotions of solitude and longing so close to the surface, she was more than ripe for a healing massage like the ones she remembered.

Every day as she left her student hostel, and every
night upon returning, she gazed at a neon sign hanging
from the top floor of a nearby condominium. It said
MASAJE in big, green, hypnotizing letters. It also said
Peluquería Los Remedios and named other services:
depilatories and facials. At night, Lola closed her eyes
and saw the green sign: MASAJE, ever expanding in
her mind. She feared that she might never receive that
which her body-mind-spirit so urgently longed for. The
problem was her student budget. Even if she sacrificed
dinner for two full weeks, it would be difficult to pay
for the extravagance she craved. But she did sacrifice
those dinners and kept doing it until, besides losing ten
pounds, she had saved up just enough money to procure
the longed-for healing of body, mind and spirit.

Finally, the day before moving on from her beloved
Sevilla, Lola climbed the stairs of the condominium
she had been stalking and entered *La Peluquería Los
Remedios*. It was a long salon, about 45 feet by 15
feet, flanked on both sides by dozens of enormous hair
dryers attached to the wall. Under each dryer there was
a lady. And, it seemed, between the feet of each lady
there was a small child or a tranquil dog. The place was
packed. No one payed much attention to her, but she
glimpsed, at the end of the tunnel, a tall, thick-waisted,
bosomy blonde lady dressed in white. Strangely big and
blonde to be a Sevillian. "That must be the masseuse,"
thought Lola hopefully. "Maybe she's a Swede! Yes!
That Swedish massage is deeply therapeutic!"

Upon finding herself in front of the blonde, Lola introduced herself, and explained that she wanted to receive a massage.

"Right away," said the Swede, with an exotically sensual accent. "Last door on the left. You can wait for us there."

When she walked through that door, Lola was surprised to see that the little room was almost completely occupied by a round, stainless steel pool filled with boiling, yellow wax. The wax made a "blu blu blu" sound, like an enormous, bubbling fish tank in slow motion. Fascinated, Lola observed the volcanic, cornmeal-colored movement before noting that – besides a hair-washing sink with a chair – the only other article in the room was a massage table without a mattress. Not even a sheet covered it. It was just a stainless steel table, like the ones she'd seen at the veterinarian's.

Lola smiled thinking about the Swede's rules of hygiene. And wanting to respect them, she kept her panties on, leaving a prudent barrier of fabric between her humid parts and the cold table. She waited a good ten minutes. It was cold. Just as she jumped off the table to cover herself, her masseuse knocked at the door.

"Come in," she answered enthusiastically, looking toward the door with her exuberant breasts in the air. But what came through the door was a long, beak-like nose, a pair of disbelieving dark eyes and the hump-backed body of an 80-something-year-old man. The old man's mouth got bigger and his eyes blinked confused, before he recovered enough strength to slam the door and yell in a voice reserved for emergencies of life or death: *"La americana está completamente desnuda!* The American is completely naked! *La americana está completamente desnuda!"*

Shocked, Lola heard the echo as one lady after another lifted the hair dryer to yell to her neighbor, communicating the astonishing message: *"Desnuda!* Naked! Naked! *La americana! Completamente desnuda!"*

Time stood still as Lola stared at the neon sign which, at that very moment was in plain view. Massage. Facials. Depilation. Oh no! Facial depilatory massage? Could *that* be the massage being offered in this room with its cold metal table and its vat of scalding, bubbling wax?

She faced the truth. She had two options of escape: a sure but painful suicide diving into the boiling vat, or a quick jump to the fire escape that awaited her just outside the window. She chose the latter option. Quickly, she pulled up her skirt and put on her shoes. As she reached for her brassiere, she noted that suddenly the salon had become extraordinarily silent. At that very moment, the Swede walked in.

Lola asked to be forgiven, understanding now the gravity of her mistake. Even in New York City, stripping down to one's panties in a beauty parlor would be newsworthy. But there during the last days of

General Franco's Spain in 1975, days of early curfews and mounted riflemen in the university halls?!

With her hands in prayer position, Lola humbly explained: "I am so sorry. In my country, I studied full-body massage and we always practiced in the nude. I understood that you offered Swedish massage, and I came for that! I have a terrible pain . . . ."

"Yes, my friend," smiled the Swede. "We studied Swedish massage, but here we do not offer body massage."

Silence.

"I am sorry. I'm sorry for having caused any bad feelings."

"Bad feelings? You simply caused a big surprise! Man oh man, did you cause a surprise! Come on. Lie down here and I'll give you your massage now."

Lola obediently lay down with her skirt and her shoes on. Her now-stiffer-than-ever back was in direct contact with the cold, shiny metal of the table, waiting for a hand that would help her release at the very least, the tensions caused by this, her latest adventure.

But the Swede knew very little about the healing arts. And frankly, before Lola's naked breasts, the esthetician felt so strange and so cold that she could only rub Lola's face with one finger, making tiny circles in rapid succession, without even looking at her client's supplicating eyes. Seven minutes later, when the cream ran out, Lola sat up on the table suddenly, like a cadaver touched by *rigor mortis*. Fighting to keep back tears of frustration, she was only able to declare to her masseuse that she needed to leave, immediately.

There was no noise at all in the main area of the beauty parlor. It would be a good moment to escape from *La Peluquería Los Remedios*. Except that the silence was one of expectation! When she opened the door, she saw not the thirty-or-so ladies, children and dogs that twenty minutes earlier had been sitting below their hot-air-blowing dryers, but about eighty or ninety people, including several men standing in uncomfortable positions on top of the hair-drying chairs, with their cameras fixed on her!

Lola walked the gauntlet with her head high, affirming in silence that her only sin had been to seek a healing of body and soul in a Sevillian beauty parlor in 1975.

On the way to her hostel, with the repeating echo of *"completamente desnuda"* still pulsing within her head, she remembered with horror the expression on the face of the old man who would surely relive their encounter on oh-so-many occasions.

Then, from the first street corner, a thin, greasy-looking man with a stray-dog type of look, shouted out to her: "Your legs are the columns of the temple . . . where I need to pray!"

"Not now!", whispered Lola, wishing with all of her soul to be invisible to all the men of Sevilla.

She looked up to the infinite sky and breathed deeply, asking for a consoling thought, some peace for her mind, for her heart, for her still trembling columns. And then, from a television set in a humble household, a simple word leapt from the window to her ears: *INOCENTE!*

What a beautiful word! Innocent! Of course! Her pure innocence had caused a memorably scandalous occurrence in a Sevillian beauty salon. Ha! Lola envisioned her friend Rudy in all of his wisdom. How he would laugh to hear this story!

Touched with gratitude, and still looking up at the sky, Lola smiled. Lola laughed. And finally, she opened her entire being to what she sometimes calls the Mystery.

Chapter four

Barefoot doctors connect

•

It's not like I lit candles for *him*. I, Eugenia
Quiñones Pérez, would never do anything to bind
someone to me. That's how *brujos* get full of
themselves and end up becoming sorcerers. No, no, no.
But I confess that I did light candles three nights before
the *bomba* dance. Girl, I lit those candles because I just
turned 40 and I don't want to die without sharing the
great Mystery that's all inside of me. And with those
candles, I asked that someone would come to me. A
man . . . a man who could handle all of me! That's it!
With each candle I asked for something: my health and
his health, my happiness and his. I had no idea who
would come, which man it would be. I didn't know if he
was already living in Almácigo or if he was on his way.
But I knew it would happen. First because in my entire
life I have hardly ever asked anything for myself. And
second, because I did it clean. Without anyone special
in mind. Just knowing that the moment had arrived.
For me and for him. And after I lit those candles, I
said at the end: "I am now ready to give and receive and
receive and give the way I know we can."

*I'm Hernán. Got home late from fishing with
Mangual and we did real nice! I took fish to everyone
in the family and we had barracuda al fogón at Mai's
house. Mai, who is still as sharp as a tack and strong
as a guayacán, thanks be to God. So it was already*

dark when I got to my place, and I felt like making a nice calalú with lots of amaranth greens. I harvested a bunch and they were in their prime with their leaves all big and beautiful.

I lit the fire and saw candles burning. At first I thought it was just a spirit passing through. But then, as I got that flame going, among the dry leaves and the kindling and the smoke that started rising, I clearly saw a woman lighting candles, and then I recognized her. It was Eugenia Quiñones!. Geña! So I sat there in front of the fire to see what was going on. I shut my eyes but I kept seeing those candles just the same. And then I saw us like in a dream, saying goodbye. "Don't worry, mi reina. Here and now they are coming to kill us. But in another place I am going to love you. You'll see. When you light your candles, I will remember this moment and I will find you wherever you may be." I was saying that to her in a dream, in another body at another time.

I might enjoy looking at those big, handsome guys, but let's face it. They are mostly so self-absorbed: "Oh, I'm so fine!" You know, just looking to find the best deal, how can they get more and more for themselves. They don't know how to listen. They don't know how to love in a humble way. And far from making life easier for a lady, they complicate every little thing. No, no, no . . . . I prefer to be single and free and happy. That's been good enough for me.

But Hernán Osorio Cosme is something else.
People are afraid of Nan because he died once and came
back to life with a smile on his lips and his hands all
soft. Now he cures those impossible cases. Yes, ma'am.
He cures those who are literally on their way out . . . if
it's right for them to live, that is.

Before that lightning bolt hit him, Elvina had
Nan under her power. Elvina and her cousin who does
"holy" spells, as they call them. For more than a year,
that woman had him bound to her. He was really tied
up good! Until that lightning bolt left him dead and
breathing. Without knowing what was going on around
him. With his eyes open but without seeing a thing.
Two months later, Elvina left him. She jumped ship,
yeah. Got herself on a boat and crossed the big ocean.
Yes indeed. And she has never again been seen around
these parts.

After more than one long year, Nan came back
from that death bed knowing things that he didn't used
to know. That scares a lot of people, but not me. No,
I understand those things. I have my protections. My
guides help me in my work with children, the hardest,
most complicated cases. Listen up, girl. And since I
was a child, I've had my eyes on that brother!

So last night, big surprise for everyone! Nan
Osorio Cosme shows up at the *bombazo*! First he
danced a nice *leró* with his sister Tita and then he came
by where I was eating a *tortilla de yuca*. He asked

me to dance a *cuembé* with him. And then a *holandé:*
Murió Amelia, Amelia, qué pasó. Murió Ameleia, se
fue y me dejó. We were dancing right by one of the
drums while María Victoria, all dressed in yellow, stole
the show. In our little corner, someone sprayed rum over
the floor. The aroma came to me: rum cured in coconut.
My feet moved to the rhythm over that hard and cool
floor of just-pressed earth. My feet, my legs, my entire
body dancing that driving, fast rhythm with words
about death among the shadows and Nan's teeth, Nan's
shoulders, Nan's eyes. And I gave myself completely to
that play of attitudes: you know, come on over, brother,
and now I could care less. That *holandé* rhythm is
savage wild.

Soon as we finished in front of the drums, he
suggested we go outside to cool off. The sugarcane
crabs were running toward the river mouth. And under
those stars, surrounded by all those crabs hitting the
stones of the road with their shells, I remembered the
rociados de yuca that I'd made that afternoon without
having a reason to. That was my sign that I could let
myself go, that in the morning we would have a fine
breakfast with strong, black coffee with just a pinch
of sugar the way Nan likes it, that is . . . if his tastes
haven't changed since his lightning death!

*I have always had eyes for that girl. It's not that
she be a knockout! If the truth be told, right now I don't
even know what she looks like on the outside. Ever*

since the lightning got me, I can only see what's inside of people. But even as a boy I remember thinking that Grandma B was the most beautiful lady in the world, and she had no teeth! Yes, my friend, Geña is a free and beautiful queen and always will be. She's an empress! She has never let herself be controlled by anyone. Ever. I still see her like when she was 11 years old. The same girl who escaped one time to traipse with me all through our barrio Almácigo searching for bird eggs and watching the swallows flying in and out of their cave and running more than I could run around all of our territory. Oh, yes. I remember that afternoon! Almost everyone was sick and there was nothing to eat at home except casabe. *Don Faustino took us to his little place. First we all cooked up a bunch of cane crabs. It was quite the stew. I still remember how good it tasted! Then we prepared* maguey *medicine right there in the* fogón. *Geña painted herself black with charcoal, saying she was pure African. She made up "the slave Librada's work songs." Don Faustino and I played rhythm on some metal drums and took turns dancing. We stayed up real late that night. They must of beat up on that girl when she got home! But that time, with everyone being so sick and so sad, it was more important to her to be with us. We were all desperately needing some fun. And we did savor that beautiful day!*

That's the same Geña who lit the candles, just as we agreed so many times ago. And now that I am free, I think our moment has arrived. If she looks at me

*with desire tonight, I'll take her off to my little shack
and I will learn to love her. Yes indeed.*

So, that night of the dance, after we walked for
a while, we got to Nan's place. He lit the lanterns and
I sat at the edge of his bed, a cedar bed he carved
himself. I felt like a queen with Nan at my side. The
night was so fragrant; it was all about cedar wood,
sugarcane, the ocean, the open sky, Nan. And that man
did not smell like rum. He was all earthy; pure vetiver
roots! I swear to you, girlfriend, he hadn't drunk a
drop of liquor!

I remember one time when we were just kids.
Everyone was sick, so Mami took all my brothers and
sisters to auntie Salomé's place. No one worried about
me, since I was healthy. So I ran off with Nan to
discover the swallows' cave, and to visit don Faustino.
Then we all cooked a cane crab stew together. It was
almost too delicious! Never forget it. Don Faustino
taught us to soften *maguey* pulp over the fire and we
mashed up its warm juice with molasses and raw onion
and a brew of sweet spices. That's the surest remedy
there is for asthma, cough, even pneumonia. Then we
toasted a mountain of *hidionda* seeds and we drank
hidionda coffee that tasted like chocolate. Faustino told
us about the swallows and the remedies he knew how
to make from their droppings in the cave. That day of
total freedom is my favorite memory of my childhood.
Playing with Nan. Imagine! They *never* let me play

with the boys. For one glorious day I'd escaped from the slavery of cleaning, washing and the eternal *burén*.

We came through my door and I felt peace. Peace, and a sensation that Geña was just right among so many plants with their aromas and that whiff of almácigo smoke smoldering in the fogón. *And then we seen what seemed like a miracle. The whole place was filled with lightning bugs!*

The lightning bugs welcomed me. When I was a little girl, the lightning bugs told me so many things: *Lightning bug, lightning bug, God bless you. Now tell me, tell me, tell me the truth!* Then if the lightning bug jumped, it was a yes, and if it didn't jump, it was a no. And those buggers filled Nan's place, jumping as if each and every flash of light was a yes and a winking eye of our people who'd passed but who were watching us!

Nan had a nice mattress made from balsa fibers, and blankets made from cotton and *maguey* strands that are scratchy and warm. Fibers from the same plants that don Faustino and Nan use for so many remedies. And among all those blinking lights, other aromas reached me: *poleo, santa maría de playa*, lightly-burned coconut oil and the sweats of our *bomba* dance.

I told her: "I'm in no hurry, mi reina. I'm in for the long run with you." So many years admiring her. So many years wishing for this sensation that has no name. I'm in no hurry at all. What I feel inside is a deliciousness of peace and confidence. "Good thing you lit those candles!"

Very good! And it didn't surprise me that he knew about the candles.

So that very wise and aromatic man began by washing my feet. Washing my feet, sister! He was the longest time massaging those feet, deep-like, with that coconut oil. Then some tickles before he moved up to my ankles, my calves. He caressed every inch of my holy calves with that nicely browned coconut oil. Talking to me all the while about the walks he wanted to go on with me by our old cave, by the river in full moon, and out until sunrise.

When he was supposed to get to my thighs, girl, he jumped up way high! Holy Mother of God! With those smoothest of hands, he delicately lowered the sleeves of my dress and worked my shoulders, caressing me with pressure and tenderness and lots of know-how around my neck. I felt those hands as if he were inside my womb, inside my bone marrow. And he stayed there a long time casting out forgotten angers and sorrows until I felt tears flowing down my face. Pure relief, sister. Relief! Then I undid the ties on my dress and that man blessed me with his healing hands on my arms, my back, all the way to my waist. Wise strokes, his strokes. They came into me like rain at the end of a long, Lenten drought.

When he got to my waist, I somehow got out
from under and turned face up. And can you believe
that that man did not stop caressing me? No, girl.
He started in on my thighs and that was pure torture
because he did not stop teasing me there although
between sighs and bad words I told him all the wicked
things I was looking forward to doing to him, and
for variety's sake, all the great dishes I was going to
prepare for him. He was just moving slow, girl. SLOW.
Sometimes, between our sweat and our pleasure, we
had to stop to laugh at my wild woman songs and my
descriptions of the dishes we so love to eat.

*Before kissing her breasts I could see she loved
me to the bone. She didn't say it but she couldn't hide it
either. No one can hide anything from me.*

When he got to my *tetas*, his hands gave me
something I have never received from any man.
Something like tenderness mixed with fever mixed with
lightning . . . and laughter! Free, loose laughter, but held
in! Delicious! And softness. As if I were one of his
plants, one of the plants he picks with what feels like
reverence, for his remedies of life or death.
    Because Nan is not a green witch, exactly. No.
But when there are matters of life and death, well since
he was alive over on the other side for a time, he knows
about all that, and he covers the person with plants and
almácigo water. *Almácigo* smoke. *Almácigo* smudges.

And the person maybe decides to live. Yeah. He works
with dying people. And when there's a dead person
trapped inside of someone, he also helps that dead
person so she can find her way. If part of a person has
gotten lost and gone away, he even knows how to free
that part from where it's hiding and helps to bring it
back home. All that is his work. He does it with great
respect and lots of love, and it is beautiful. He said he
could teach me some of his ways to help me with the
children who come to me.

So while that brother is making me twist and
shout and tremble and laugh, I'm seeing visions and
remembering other times in other places. That's how I
know that all of this is from now and also from before,
and that's how – without thinking about Nan at all – I
was able to call him to me with my candles and my
gratitude.

*Then that good woman jumped on top of me and
took me into her insides and played with me real fine,
telling me things I will never repeat, and she wasn't the
Geña of now but the Geña of where I have been without
being able to tell you where it is, that place. I saw us at
a big bombazo and then in a hammock among maguey
plants and swallows flying. And then we were like
two cats fighting for our lives. So much, so much pure
pleasure!*

We left Nan's place to cool off and ran like two children in the half light of dawn to fetch those *rociados de yuca* before Fidelia and auntie Salomé found them. We ended up on Rubí Beach, where we bathed a bit and fished out a pair of lobsters from the rocks for our supper. Then we went back to bed!

That afternoon, we smoked a little artemisia. Then, right as we were preparing some *almácigo* broth for our blood, I realized that next to this man who died and came back from that place with a clear vision of the truth, I could be free. Free! That word, the most beautiful I know. Free, beneath those hands softened and toned by aromatic roots of pepperseed, *oronés* and lemon grass. Free! What I have always wanted. Ha! They have ridiculed me plenty for wanting freedom!

And now, at 40 years old and feeling tender and in peace with myself and with the Mother of God, I am grateful for my faith. Because in spite of what they all said, and in spite of so much criticism, being alone for so many years, I never gave up. I never felt it was too late. I didn't go with any old man so as not to be alone. I maintained my faith that I could have a life shared my way, among all that I love the most, and for the very greatest good of our people.

Chapter five

Twins

•

That peculiar morning, in the entire *barrio* of Piñales, the cows started their day looking toward the east. The roosters didn't crow. The chickens didn't cluck. The doves didn't coo. Even the *coquíes* forgot to sing.

Inside that silence, I saw for the first time, big black birds like giant swallows with their scissor tails half-way open, flying over our mountains. *"Tijerillas en tierra,"* said Pai. And then I remembered that saying: *"Tijerilla en tierra, tormenta en la mar."*

Tormenta!

"Hurricane," said Pai without hardly moving his lips. His face got stiff. He looked skinnier and more tired than ever. Mai looked at him over the baby's head. Then she looked at me and she pressed Luisa to her breast so she could eat, but she wasn't crying and she didn't want any milk. It started to rain. I looked at the cracks between the palmwood planks of our floor. I heard a long sigh. Then a whirlpool of nervous feelings started moving from my feet to my belly. I wanted to do something and I didn't know what to do.

This house won't take it," said Pai.

I didn't want to hear more. I ran quick to where my twin brother Nacho was, and I said, real nervous like: "Hurricane's coming!" Nacho shrugged his shoulders and he looked at me with his hands open as if to say: "Nothing we can do about it."

Then Pai and Mai and the little ones left the house in single file. "We're going to Tomasa's place," yelled Pai. Nacho and I got in line without a word. I felt Nacho very serious walking behind me, protecting me, and I was grateful for that. We were both very brave, but I loved to feel protected by him. When we were together in any danger, Nacho was my hero, like in the stories that Pai would tell us when he got home from the cigar factory.*

Tomasa was our main midwife, and her house was the newest of all Piñales. It was made from the same palm wood, but it had a shiny tin roof and a windbreak made of trees toward the east and the north, where the heavy winds and rains always came from. To get there, we waked through the big tobacco field and later the sugar cane field, and then the other lands with their leaves of *yautía*, pumpkin, *malanga* and *lerenes*. Then we went past the plantain fields and the orange and lemon trees and the mango and mamey and breadfruit trees. Then we had to walk through the grasslands where Tomasa and the Rovira family had their cows and oxen and their horses, all separated by living fences made by the spiny *maya* plants and, near the river, by bamboo.

The rain drops that fell on us were so big that we got soaked in seconds. And it wasn't coming from the northeast or the south like always. It was coming from

the west. How strange! The bamboos began to bend
and bend lower and lower, as if they wanted to touch
their heads to the river and the grass. Because now
it wasn't just rain. Now it was a wind too, and it was
getting louder.

"Coming from the west!", said Pai with Juan José
in his arms when he looked at the wind break of trees
just to the north and to the east of Tomasa's house.
He looked like he was wanting to move on, but there
we all were!

The rain was falling so hard on that roof that the
people inside didn't hear us and Pai nearly broke down
the door before they opened it for us. What a surprise
to see that in that little house there were already about
40 people taking up all the space on the floor, in the
hammocks and at the table.

"Come on in! Come on in!", yelled Tomasa, happy
as if it were a party. "If the kitchen goes a flying, we
will have eaten. Thanks to our Blessed Mother, there's
food for everyone." And the next thing was that each
one of us had a calabash bowl full of a *sancocho* that
was almost black from all the purslane leaves. It was
glorious, I remember. It even had salty pork.

After we ate, someone gave a chair to Mai, who
was holding Luisa, the baby, in her arms. Berta, who
was seven, stayed close to Mai. Pai stayed with Toñín
and Juan José, who were all standing. Nacho and I
gripped our hands together for a moment before he

went over to be close to Pai and the boys. I took my place near Mai.

The sound of the rain on the roof was so loud that we couldn't even talk. At that moment, I thought that the hurricane wasn't going too badly. I felt good in that house with so many people I knew and my whole family all together, almost quiet. Lots of oil lanterns and candles were lighting up the space, so it was warm inside.

But little by little, the wind started to scream above the sound of the rain, and I understood for the first time what a monster was. That wind was a monster.

Then the smell of so many people and the sound of the wind monster killed the happiness, and I started to feel something else that I don't know its name. I thought I was going to faint, feeling so dizzy and wanting to scream. Mai and I sat there in silence but other people were yelling to one another and their voices sounded like metal grating and screeching on metal. Voices as hard as the tin roof. I didn't understand anything.

Then we started to hear something so big that we all got quiet. It was as if that monster was just outside our door, knocking everything down: knocking down the walks, knocking down the roof. Nacho came over to me and took my hand again. Everyone was real quiet and then we began to pray, all together: "Hail Mary, full of Grace . . ." I tried to see our Mother of Miracles in front of the house with her arms open toward us. But when I closed my eyes to call on her, there was another sound, like a hundred men yelling all at once: Fuuuu!

And then there was light! That good, shiny roof flew away, all in one piece. Suddenly, we were all under the sky and all that rain.

With Juan José over his shoulder, Pai held on to Toñín. Tonín took Berta's hand; Berta held on to Nacho, who was still holding my hand. I looked for Mai, who was with Luisa, and all eight of us went running toward the grasslands that separated us from our home with its palm thatched roof. And what we came across there was like a dream, where everything is backwards. Whole trees were flying like giant animals with wings. The trees were flying!

We tried to walk but it was so dangerous that after a little while, Pai hunched down and lay in the grass on the east side of a little hill. We all crouched down next to him. Pai first, face down, a little higher than Mai, who lay on her side with Luisa at her breast. Pai held on to Juan José with his arms and stuck Toñín under his left leg. Berta stayed under his right leg. Pai yelled something to Mai and she raised her calves so I could get under them. I screamed because I saw Nacho crawling to get away from us. I didn't want him to go. But he had seen the stump of a mango tree that was budding in two places. He perched himself between the two new branches and there he stayed, way above the mud. I felt torn in two. I wanted to be with Nacho. He was always so brave.

Then Nacho, in the mango tree, and the rest of us spread out over the earth, well we caught that rain. We took that water and heard that furious monster wind. We could feel the earth move every time a tree fell or a flying tree trunk got stopped with a crash to the earth or against another tree or a rock. I kind of got used to being on the ground, holding on to the grass, its roots, the stones. I had never felt so much water on my body. Cold water with so much noise, like anger, an anger bigger than people's anger. The wind was angry that day and I remembered, in Paí's stories, that for the Indians, that monster of the wind had a name. Jurakán! A devil. Or a God. Or both.

Little by little I got calm. I felt safe under Mai's legs; they moved a lot. She was still lying on her side so she could feed Luisa. The rain was as hard as the waterfall at Charco Negro. And cold! It was a long night. It lasted like one whole year of suffering, even though at one point I stopped feeling it all. I stopped feeling the drops of water. I think I even fell asleep a little.

When that long night ended, the wind wasn't blowing much but it was still raining. We could hear the cows calling, mooing with that sad sound of pain and desperation that made all my hairs stand on end. They were crying out to be milked. Then we got up as we could, bit by bit. I was shivering. Toñín was shaking a *lot*. Berta was crying. The littlest ones, Luisa and Juan José, were better off, since they had spent the night in Mai's and Pai's arms. It was not easy to get ourselves up off the ground and walk because we were stiff and covered with mud. Our clothes were so heavy! I was almost crawling over to where Nacho had spent the night. I tried to run but I fell over and over again. There I was, so anxious to see my brother. I called him: "Wake up, Nacho! The hurricane is over! Wake up!"

Finally we arrived. We found him sitting in the crotch of that mango tree but another tree's trunk had fallen on top of him. It had fallen on his chest. He was dead. My beloved brother was dead! My best friend, my hero. Dead! I screamed and screamed. Like in a nightmare, I screamed in desperation and I could not run. I could hardly move. I wanted to leave my body to be with my brother. Mai said some prayers and her voice trembled. Pai lowered Juan José from his shoulder and gave him to me so that he could try to move that tree trunk. My arms were trembling. Pai struggled for a long time with that tree trunk but he couldn't move it. He cried. I think it was because he was so mad, losing his first-born son, and giving that tree trunk all of his strength for nothing. I was crying. Juan José was screeching in my arms. We all cried. Mai with Luisa at her breast without moving. Finally, Pai said: "Noone can help us today. Tomorrow I'll get the guys to come and we'll bury him at home."

Then we turned around. We were all so sad, and shaking and falling again and again, stripping off our clothes little by little so we could move. That's how we walked without Nacho under the rain to our house.

We were so close, and yet we took over an hour to get there. Everything was different. There were lots of fallen trees. The river had formed a swamp that covered the lower fields. We couldn't cross it. We had to go up the Roviras' hill. And when we finally got home, we saw that just behind the house, where there had always been a wall of trees and earth, suddenly we could see all of barrio Almácigo and up to the sea.

We were all surprised to see that half of our roof was still there. Our Mother of Miracles was there without moving from her spot on top of the closet, although for the first time, the oil candle that always lit up Her corner was dark.

There wasn't a piece of *almácigo* or any dry wood, and the roof of the *fogón* was gone. Mai took down some green-leaf moonshine from the closet. She took off the rest of our wet and heavy clothes and she rubbed us all down with her liniment. It smelled so very good; it was full of *malagueta* leaves and *ruda* and lots of tobacco leaves. Mai rubbed us hard and then we jumped up and down for a while to get warm.

Pai went to where the goat and the cows were calling, and under that rain he milked them and brought us all warm milk. Then, while Mai gathered some sweet potatoes and *yautías* that had fallen from the wood stove, I was shocked to see that Pai was hacking away at our good kitchen table with his machete so we could cook. That's the last thing I remember of that day. I fell asleep on the floor there, and they say I slept for a whole week. No one could wake me.

Could it be that I died a little so I could be with Nacho? The truth is that I didn't want to live without him.

Then I started feeling that he was inside of me. He would talk to me. He said lots of things, sometimes nice things. But I didn't want to help around the house any more. I didn't want to take care of the animals. I was supposed to take care of the little kids. I did it, but I was mean to them. The only thing I wanted was to hear Nacho's voice, and he only talked to me when we were alone. I stopped being a good girl. When Mai asked me to cook something, no one liked what I made. Everything I cooked up tasted bad. Real bad!

One morning almost a year after the hurricane, Pai threw his plate of my tasteless, half-raw cornmeal breakfast on the floor. He got up, grabbed me by the hair and looked into my eyes for the longest time. I was scared. I thought maybe Pai could see the only desire that tormented me day and night. When he let me loose, he took my hand. Then he looked at Mai with her giant belly and the green tobacco poultice she was wearing around her forehead and he said: "I'm taking her right now to Almácigo and may our Holy

Mother protect her. Since the hurricane, this girl is not
worth a sliver of cow dung."

I thought they were going to leave me in another
barrio, that they were going to sell me. And for the
first time since the hurricane, I was afraid for my life.
But Pai wasn't a bad man. I was his oldest daughter.
It wasn't possible that they would sell me. "Don't sell
me!", I yelled. Pai took me by the arm and he looked
into my eyes again. *"Mi hija*, calm down," he said, softly.
"We are going to cure you." And then he set me up on
the spotted mare with him, and I didn't feel my brother
while that mare walked down the mountain path,
shaking all of my body and my mind with every step.

We finally reached barrio Almácigo. It smelled of
the sea there, and of a nice *fogón*, with its wood smoke,
kitchen smoke. We went through a little dirt road till
we got to the *batey* of a house made of palm thatch and
yaguas with a big open kitchen just outside. Pai greeted
the lady, who had lovely, shiny, dark-coffee-with-milk-
colored skin. She was dressed in white. She had tied
her black hair in two braids around her head. She smiled
real pretty. They talked for a while, and then the lady,
Geña is her name, she came over to me. First she burned
some branches of rosemary while she said some prayers.
Then she made a cross and some other signs in the air
in front of me and she looked very long at my eyes. But
it wasn't like when Pai did it. When doña Geña looked
into my eyes I felt peaceful and safe. Then she started
speaking to me for a long time and I rested even more.
In my dreamy state, I heard her asking me a long

question that ended with what was my name. And to my surprise, I said "Nacho."

"Nacho," she said. "You are here with your beloved sister Abelarda. You died during the hurricane and you were supposed to leave this world. But Nacho, you love your sister so much that you decided to stay with her. You stayed here within her body, within her mind. Now, Nacho, I have come to explain to you that you are hurting your sister Abelarda. I know that you love her. I have come to tell you that without wanting to, you are doing her great harm. Listen to me, Nacho. Since you live within her, she is always confused. She can't live her life. And you can't live what *you* should be living. Because you should be at the side of all the saints and angels and your grandparents and all the other ancestors who love you and are waiting for you so that, from heaven, you can keep on learning and helping the people on this side . . . ."

I don't remember everything she said to me, I mean to Nacho. I felt a little dumb, half-asleep, like. But suddenly, I woke up and saw him in front of me, saying goodbye. His head wasn't all bloody like when I'd seen him under that tree trunk. He was serious, but he looked healthy. He kissed me on the forehead. Then, brave and true as ever, he turned around and walked away. The next thing was I woke up as if I had been dreaming. I felt sick so I got up and ran to a pile of yam and plantain and banana peels and threw up that awful cornmeal cereal I'd made. Then I felt light.

Pai took me in his arms and laid me down in
a hammock. Then doña Geña gave me a nice tea of
guanábano and sour orange leaves with a dark piece of
cane sugar. It was real good. Pai looked serious but
his face was soft. He was drinking his tea. Lots of
roosters were crowing.

Then a handsome, smiling, dark coffee-colored
man with a fine, tightly woven palm hat came by.
After a little talking, Pai gave him a bunch of cigars.
Then Pai gave doña Geña a gallon of alcohol with lots
of malagueta and ruda leaves and plenty of tobacco.
That smiling man gave Pai a nice string of snapper
fish. And we all four of us said our goodbyes.

Doña Geña gave me her hands and I squeezed
them. Then I did something I had never done before,
but that Pai always told us in the stories of the royal
queens. I kneeled down before her and I kissed her
hands. They smelled like coconut oil. And I felt fine.

Lots of tears fell from my eyes as we returned
home on that mare. I felt sorry because I knew that
my brother was suddenly really far away. But it didn't
hurt me too much. Something was right. *I* felt right.

Suddenly, I was anxious to see my little sisters
and brothers and all the animals. I wanted to help
Mai out with everything. She needed me bad! She was
pregnant, and so very sad, ever since the hurricane.

Chapter six

Cokaine

•

LOLA:

Sometimes we think it's easy to recognize a drug
addict. Because we see lots of homeless people with
needle marks, all wasted and begging on the corners
and we think that's how drug addicts are. But not all
of them! Some are lawyers, actors, police. And they
go to work everyday. Some go to the gym three or four
times a week. Some are real good looking. They go
to the dermatologist. For everything that goes wrong,
there's a pill. And they keep their figures and they get
expensive haircuts and present an attractive persona.
Some make believe they have a relationship with a
person called 'friend.' And they charm you with an
irresistible talk, talk, talk . . . They tell you stories,
they look at you in that way . . . . They play with your
feelings. They get you to fall in love, alright. But as
time goes on, you see those quick changes, you feel
that something is not right, and you ask the question.
Then they look at you with their deeply offended
look: "But baby, I don't use *any* drugs. None!" You,
with the doubt eating you from within, you try to
convince yourself: "It's true that when he's with me he
doesn't even drink much." So then you think that the
distraction might be another woman . . . or another
man . . . or that he simply doesn't love you. I mean,
he loves having you in his life because you represent
a healthy type of pleasure, or because you make his

life easy and you share with him beautiful times in the mountains, among waterfalls: different types of experiences, clean. But he doesn't take the initiative to create anything between you. And he changes his plans at the last moment. And he invites you and then un-invites you. And he doesn't call when he says he will. And he won't spend the night. He's always out of here by 10 pm, ear stuck to his telephone, walking fast toward the alleyway.

JAVI

One capsule of crack costs $8 in the street, but you can smoke up 13, 15, 18 rocks in one night . . . and the next day, you go to work. No one notices anything because no one wants to believe that you, such a good guy, are using crack. What I notice is that the conversations don't go where they're supposed to go. When I want to impress with just the right words, the words I want don't come to my mind. And if you all watched closely, you would see that I have to fight all the time to stay awake . . . and I never go to the john. My intestines are all dried up.

Thank God, I got a little day job doing security in a parking lot. So I don't have to make much conversation. Working there, nobody notices my laziness. I got no energy. I ain't worth a dime. Sometimes I drink coffee or those sweet drinks with lots of caffeine to give me energy . . . or I take diet pills so I don't nod off during the day. At night, all I

want to do is smoke my rocks. I'm not smoking much
right now because I have my lady and her children,
and I want to help them get ahead. So every once in
a while I hold off and go down to two or three rocks.
It's not a high that lasts. If you eat something, it all
vanishes. All the money you spent gets thrown away
when you eat, even if you just nibble a little something.
But if I don't smoke, I get sick. And with just one
draw, all of my problems vanish. And I feel good for a
while. Not good; great! I live to feel that!

MAGO

I know I'm not doing too great, but I pay the
rent and I go to work. I even save some money! I go
to church. I go to the retreats. I get on my knees. I
ask Jesus to guide me, to watch over me. He gives me
peace. But at the end of the day, the best peace of all
is the one I get sniffing up some coke. That's the real
thing!

The best of all is to go to church high. It's a
sensation that everything is clean, that everything
shines with its own light. Nothing hurts! I know that
as time goes on, it's taking its toll; but coke makes me
so brilliant! My body feels powerful. I want to run
five miles, six, eight! I used to run all that and more,
but I fucked up my knee pretty bad, so now I go to the
gym and I walk on the machine. I keep my legs looking
fine, that's for sure. I keep them shaved and shiny.
Yeah. Well, like I was saying. When I don't have my

lady Blanca, I feel sick. Headache. Every ache. I can't even think straight.

I had a good friend. She took me to some beautiful places and she was even teaching me to dance, but she wanted me like a boyfriend. You know, calling her and wanting to know how things were going. But with the calls I have to make to my kids and my connections, that's enough. I don't need any more obligations during the week. I hate feeling I *have* to do something. Anything!

She left me. *Perico* helped me to keep her around more than once. I would tell her lots of stories and you know, when you got *perico* in your blood, your words are unstoppable. And just right! But after about six months, she would cry every time we spoke, begging me to tell her the truth. She knew something wasn't right, but she had no idea. She thought I had another lady. HA! I couldn't deal with her alone! She had nice legs, a nice body. She would have loved me right. But I wasn't straight with her. What can you do? Lose if you tell, lose if you don't tell. Now I want to hook up with a younger babe. No tears! A sweet young thing who just wants to have fun. Crazy fun!

JAVI

With crack, well you know, I don't have relations with my lady. I think she's going to leave me. I'm always in my room because I can't deal with her kids. They don't respect me. So I put on music in my "cave" and smoke a few rocks so I don't feel all that bad being there. But after I shower, that high just disappears and everything is the same, even if I've smoked three or four rocks. If she leaves me, I'll go back to my town. There, there's no crack, just cokaine. It's another scene in my town. So I'll be with cokaine because I can't be without anything with the problems I have. I mean, I got problems!

What do you mean *what* problems? The worst days are the days I get paid. Every time I think I'm gonna have that money in my hands, I get sick, man. Sick to my gut. And when I have the money in my pocket and go to cop my rocks, I get nauseous real bad! It's like panic! Sometimes I'm walking toward the *punto*, and I have to stop on the way to vomit. I hate that! But with the first little toke, all of those bad feelings just disappear and I feel good again. Sometimes I think it would be better if I wasn't addicted, but for now, crack is what I love.

They sent me for treatment, but what they give is advice! If they gave me something to take, well that would be alright. But they just want to talk and talk. I'm not going because I lost my car and I get tired walking. That center is about five blocks from my house. I'm 37 years old and I get tired so fast!

EDÍN

I worked with addicts in jail. That's where you see the cokaine! Cokaine, heroin, crack. It's all there!

You see it all 'cause lots of employees are using, and they control plenty of inmates with drugs. When I worked there, I wasn't using any drugs at all. I even stopped smoking cigarettes because I have two kids, a little boy and a girl, and I want to be a good example for them. And with all that I know about the dangers ... But sometimes you do strange things! So much talk of drugs, so much suffering for drugs. "Must be like love," I would think to myself. "Must be so good that people will sacrifice anything to have it." And that thought was working on me. I wanted to try it one time just to kill my curiosity. But not with the people at work. With them, never!

One day a friend from New York came to see me and we went walking along the beach. He offered me cokaine. I will never forget that night! My friend showed me how to use it and left me enough for four lines in a little bottle before going off to see his family. So I would stop every so often, sniff up his little gift, and then get back to walking on the beach. And I swear that the ocean was breathing with me! I was breathing with the ocean! That beach was empty, but if there had been any bad guys lurking about, I wouldn't have been afraid of them. I wouldn't have been afraid of anything. I felt true ecstasy! The moon was full. All of my senses were on high. I felt the smell of the ocean in my body, for real! The sound of the wind in the palms was the most beautiful music I had ever heard. I began to sing and my voice sounded incredible! I invented two whole songs. Two songs

in one night, my friend! Two hits! And that's how I
spent the most enlightened night – and morning – of
my life. But I will never touch *perico* again. The next
day I discovered deep depression. Literally, I could not
get out of bed. I didn't want to. I couldn't! I felt a
heaviness in my body. A heaviness and an emptiness!
The only thing I could think was: "If I had just a little
bit more, I could do it all. Just a tiny bit more!" I
started dragging myself along the floor to call my
friend. *YO!* And then I stopped myself cold. I didn't
go to my rehab job that day. I stayed in bed with a
low and dirty feeling. Wishing I felt different. And
you know, a thousand times one little thought passed
through my mind: "How easy it is to get stuck on doña
Blanca!"

WALTER

When you fall in love with Blanca, there's no
one can compare to her! You could give a damn about
nothing. Except her! She just makes you feel so good
in every way. It doesn't matter what kind of problems
you might have. But then, since you begin having more
and more problems, you need her more and more. The
first time is something that I could never explain.
It is the most divine! The most perfect! You know.
Then you keep looking for that same feeling, that same
experience. But you can never get it back sniffing the
stuff, even if you spend a fortune. So you decide to
try shooting it up. That's better. Because you feel that

perfect high again. But it doesn't last long. It lasts such a short time! You have to keep shooting up and shooting up every 10 or 15 minutes. A few weeks ago I gave myself about 40 shots, searching for a vein, a vein. I'm not gonna tell you where I finally ended up, my friend. Yeah. In that really big, nice juicy vein. Incredible, right? First and last time! Because that blood didn't stop flowing. And later on, the pain was unbearable!

When I don't have money, I just wait on the corner until someone gives me the signal. There is so much cokaine in the street. I don't have to wait too long before someone will give me some coke for just a little bit of me. Women . . . and men too! But I'll be clear about this. I'm not anyone's girl. Get that straight. I'm always the guy. That's how I avoid Aids and I know I'm no addict. I've got my principles. Become a *doña* for a piece of the *doña*. Ha! That would be the end, right?

MARU

When I lived with Alejandro, I wanted to disappear. He was such a good looking guy, and beautiful inside, too. But he had a habit. He fought it. He went to his meetings, sometimes three or four times a week. But he couldn't keep a job. And although he had the best intentions and he gave his all at those meetings, he kept using. It was terrible for Ale, and for me too, but I didn't have any idea of what was going on. I was so ignorant. Innocent, he would say. Once, he needed money so bad, he actually drilled holes in our bedroom wall and started charging the neighbors to let them watch us at night. What did I know? Ale would put the music real loud, get out that mirror . . . and we'd get to work! Eventually he started taking bets!

Alejandro was a good lover. He knew all about control. And his intensity! He would say things to me that even now, just remembering his words, I get all bothered. I would sing and scream. That man got to the marrow of these bones. I loved the way he could make me feel with his words. He knew how to touch me. And in spite of all that, I spent almost every day I was with him, fantasizing about the best way to kill myself. I chose the ocean because once I just about drowned and, to tell you the truth, it was not too bad at all. I became part of the ocean, as if I only existed to be embraced by that great Grandmother of life. I let myself go. I felt the love of the sea toward me. Just before I blacked out, some surfers rescued me on a board. I still remember how I had felt so very small, like a bubble, within something so very great, Grandmother ocean.

When Ale began to get violent with me, sex got more and more intense, and I got sick. I bled for months. Then I asked him to leave and he moved back to his town. I think he really did love me and he knew he was in a bad state. Imagine how I felt when

I discovered the holes in our bedroom wall. The wife
of one of my neighbors told me all about it. I put the
light on in my room and we went out to the balcony.
We lifted up Alejandro's old shaving mirror on the
wall, and I looked through the holes that my neighbor
showed me in *my* little house. I couldn't even speak.
No wonder I wanted to drown myself, and I never
understood why.

ALEJANDRO

I'm not a bad person, but yes, I have done some
bad things. When I was a crackhead, I would do
anything to get it. In my town there was a guy who
would pay us to kill people. He gave us LOTS of rocks
and he would put on the most violent music you could
imagine. And then on a giant screen he would have
the most intense scenes. We would have to watch it
all. I don't know where he got that material. Rapes,
tortures, homicides! Raw, raw, raw! Then we would
go out and kill people we didn't even know, just to get
our crack up front and – for one full month – all we
wanted, no problems. In that violent state, I raped
women too. I don't like to use that word to describe
what I did, but I did that. I did a lot of harm.

I finally left that behind. My parents sent me
to an expensive rehab program and I graduated from
there. I wanted to stop doing those things. I got a
good job, and it was just too easy to move on up to
cokaine. Then I started doing bad things to people I

did know. My girlfriends! I ended up fucking one of
them up for life. It wasn't my intention. I just sniffed
too much coke and I wanted to last all night. I took
a little blue pill and I put *perico* all over my works,
you know. Then I put one of those films on and I gave
it to her for hours. I fucked her up bad. She bled for
months. I don't understand how she didn't know what
was going on. She didn't want to know, I say. And
that's called innocence. Or ignorance!

That's why I say you got to be smart. Wise! I
have my daughter real smart. Because if you're that
innocent, man, the world fucks with you, man. The
whole world fucks you over!

MAGO

When you work in the film industry, there's a
lot of drugs. Drugs, infidelity, a lot of things that at
first, well I was in shock. But I really admired the
stars I worked with, so I didn't walk away. On the
contrary! This *jíbaro* from barrio Piñales was down to
get inside that inner circle. Two or three lines in the
bathroom in the morning, a few more in the afternoon,
and sometimes after work with . . . well I'm not going
to name names. They're all well known. The truth is
that I destroyed my marriage with the drugs and all
my affairs.

I would like to say that I'm good at my job. I
tell people I'm the best. But deep inside, I know I'm

pretty beat. And what we produce is mostly garbage. It doesn't mean anything.

I had a beautiful childhood in agriculture. I wasn't born for the life I'm living, and while I keep going on and on, there is no way I'll be born again. And I want to be. I want to start over! In church I feel that I might be getting close. But then as soon as I get home, I go running after the *pinpin* that takes all my troubles away. Ha!

Sometimes I think of getting right, going into rehab. But then I tell myself: "Your life is good. You have what you need to live on and you are not going to start again at 60 years old. What for?" You know, beyond my work, I have no responsibilities. And I don't want them. No way! Except for my kids. I'm a grandfather now! Who would believe that?

People say I look young, but my health isn't good. I never used to get sick. But now, a thousand aches and pains. I spend a lot of my time seeing doctors: the urologist, the internist, the physical therapist. Thank God I have a good health plan. If it weren't for that plan! I pray for something different in my life and I'm stuck on Jesus. Whatever happens to me, he gives me peace. Jesus is holding me right by the hand so . . . we'll see what happens.

Chapter seven

Broken spirit

•

My name is Manuel Milagros. Manuel Miracles!
That's an ironic name, right? They call me Mago. I'm
not supposed to be sneaking into this book 'cause I
don't even like to read *or* write. So what am I doing
here? Thing is, the "author" let me talk twice already
but I want to try again, my way, without her asking no
questions. My way. Because I don't like what I said
the first time around and she won't let me change a
word of it. And if I don't tell you this story, I'm gonna
go even more crazy. So this is like a therapy for me.
And maybe somebody out there can find me some help.
There's gotta be people out there like in the old days
who understand these things. So I got this pencil in
my hand and you just correct whatever I write that's
wrong. Hear that, Benedetti?

I'm already 60 years old. All the psychologists
and psychiatrists want me to talk about my childhood,
as if that was when something terrible happened to
cause what's wrong with me, which has no name. But I
tell them all that my childhood was beautiful. Period.
We all worked together on the farm. I spent my free
time at the river with my friends. I wish to God that
all the children of today could live what I lived in the
60s in Piñales. That's not the problematic part.

What happened? Agriculture just disappeared
and the factories moved in to take its place. My older
brothers started working in the factories. My sisters

97

too. Then it was construction. So they all started
in that. Even my father went into construction and
abandoned the farm. That's when I want to start
talking about. When Papi left the farm. Around then.

I loved Papi so much. After Mami, he was the
person I loved the most. Without a doubt, he was the
person I most admired. More than anyone in this
world. When I was a kid, they said I was Calixto's
shadow. Ha! Papi gave me my nickname: Mago. That's
something. I think that of all the nine kids he had
with Mami, I was his favorite.

Papi – I called him Pai – and his brother uncle
Daniel, they taught me to plant tobacco, which is
what we were planting for a living in my *barrio* in the
50s, the 60s and even up till the 70s. Drying those
little seeds under the sun. Preparing the earth and
maintaining those ditches to drain away the water from
any heavy rains that might fall. Covering up those
baby plants to protect them, and then thinning them
out to replant them. Weeding them when they started
growing. You had to be really careful pulling those
weeds, man. Because our tobacco leaves couldn't be
damaged. You really had to take it easy! Not everyone
had permission to do that part. I did! I was an expert
working under those tobacco plants. When I was still a
little kid, Papi would say: "Mago, you are the only guy I
trust to weed that tobacco field."

I was also an expert at finding those tobacco
worms. Pai would have me search and search among

98

those plants until I got rid of them all. Because every single tobacco leaf, well we had to care for it as if it represented the entire future of our family, you see. Each and every tobacco leaf had to be harvested beautiful! Perfect!

Then, at just the right time, we had to prune those mature plants. Later, we had to harvest the leaves, all in their different stages: foot, middle, *corona*, *boliche*. And take them to the barn. We always worked together: Pai, my brothers and I.

From first grade on, I would run all the way home from school to gobble down my food and then hurry out into the fields with the men's lunch pails. I would stay out there with the men, learning about tobacco cropping and handling the oxen. I loved those animals. Pai taught me to understand them, to take care of them. To put on and take off their yoke. To guide them while they tilled the ground. To give them their grass. Those oxen have to rest; they have to drink water, and you have to feed them well. If not, if you don't give them what they need, they literally work themselves sick and they lay down and die working in the field, yoked to their partner. Sacrificed to their labor! Those animals are truly noble beings, man. Animals are better than people sometimes.

At harvest time, we all worked in the tobacco barn. We would spend the whole day walking from the field to the barn, from the barn to the field. Cutting the tobacco leaves, hanging them up to dry or sewing

them together. I didn't like to sew much because I
would stick myself with those giant needles. But when
it had to be done, well, everbody did it. All hands to
work! *¡Manos a la obra!* Later, we would take those
bunches of leaves we'd sewn together and hang them
from the rafters. That took long days of work. Whole
days hanging up those thousands of tobacco leaves to
dry, just right.

Papi and uncle Daniel built a little outdoor
kitchen, a *fogón*, right next to the barn, and Mami
would cook *guanimes de maíz con coco* and *guábara*
broth, or beans from the garden with new *yautía* leaves
and fresh, toasted rice. Corn, *gandules*, pumpkin,
sweet potatoes, *yuca*, plantains, rice . . . you know,
everything we used to eat back then.

Papi was a big partier. He played percussion:
bongo drums, güiro, maracas, everything. He played
great, and I'm not kidding. He improvised with
all the musicians who came to our neighborhood at
Christmas time. *Everybody* wanted to play with Pai.
Wherever there was a party, my father was there in
the middle of things. On our little hill, we could hear
him from anywhere in Piñales. From the other side of
the river we could listen to the best bongo player in
our territory, as Mami would say. She would tell us:
"Listen to your dad playing over at Moncho's house!"
And we would all feel proud of him. There were
times when I was so proud to be the son of Calixto
Narváez Díaz, well I could hardly fit inside my own

body I was so proud. But I also felt sad for Abelarda.
Mami suffered because, from the time of the factories,
sometimes Pai didn't come home at night even when he
was really close by. He would show up in the morning
still drunk. I don't like to say it because he was my
father and I loved him. But it's the truth. Mami
suffered big time.

Precisely speaking, that is what I want to tell you
about. Because my nightmare begins there. No one
knows this story. I have never talked about this with
anybody. But I confess it to you guys who are reading
this and who don't know me, and if you judge me I
won't find out about it. On the contrary! You might
send me a prayer so I can find the person who can
help me. I would be way thankful for that. Because
the very thing that failed me that day – the day of the
story that I'm going to tell you – well it keeps failing
me. That's how it is, and every day it gets worse.
Calixto used to say that a man is as good as his word.
That the word of a man is the measure of his worth.
And I say *¡coño, carajo!* Because if that's true, then
I'm totally worthless. What a fucked up way to live!

OK, so the story. I'm getting to the story. One
day, my father came home after my brothers had left
for the factories or for construction, whatever they
were doing. I was at home because the night before,
Grabi, Cheo and I had drunk an entire bottle of
uncured moonshine that we robbed from don Cholo,
haha. Cholo always buried his bottles in a clearing in

the forest right by the river. He was dumb enough to
bury them when the moon was full. Because we guys
were all down to try that rum. We put a wood panel up
in the *algarroba* tree and from there we watched him
drain that alcohol from the still. We were quieter than
if we were in church. Much quieter! And we saw where
he buried those bottles. We were all about 14 years
old. That night we got drunker and sicker than I ever
thought possible. And in the morning I was so dizzy,
I couldn't go to school, although Cheo passed by the
house and whistled like always. He must have drunk a
lot less than he let on.

The thing is that my father got home around ten
thirty in the morning. Mami was cooking in the *fogón*,
that woodstove kitchen, next to the house. Papi asked
for his lunch. Mami told him to hold on, that lunch
would be ready by noon, as always. Then Papi began to
yell at her, telling her that she was no good, that if he
– who provided for the family and for all the children
that she had brought in to the world – got home, and
there was nothing to eat, then she was worth nothing.
She was a lazy bitch . . . .

Whenever my father came home drunk to yell
at her, Mami got totally humble. She never reacted.
Sometimes, that strategy worked so that Papi would
turn around and just walk away, yelling to himself.
But that day, he seemed to be bothered by the way
Mai just kept peeling and cutting the *yuca*, the *ñame*,
placing them in the pot, mashing up the peppers with
the *culantro* in her *pilón*.

"Or maybe you don't have my food ready because you're out all night whoring around the neighborhood," he said to hurt her.

I felt those words cutting through my body like poison arrows. I was mad, really mad, and I felt sicker and dizzier than ever. I got up and walked to the entrance of the *fogón*. My saliva tasted sour, like vinegar in my mouth. I couldn't believe my father had said that about my mother. To begin with, for all of us and for the entire *barrio*, Abelarda was like a saint. Cooking for nine kids and in charge of growing just about everything we ate, and taking care of the animals, and sewing and washing and ironing all of our clothes. She was even the neighborhood doctor whenever anybody needed one.

"Whoring around?", I asked in silence. "Why did he say that?"

"You're all dried up. No good for nothing. Not even for cooking! Stinking whore!", he yelled.

So then Mai got tired and she said pretty loud: "I *am* cooking. And we all know that you're the one who's doing the whoring, with your girlfriends everywhere you go. I care for you and I feed your children. I work this land every day to give them food. I make and wash and sew up everyone's clothing, and God knows what diseases you bring into my bed from right there under those handsome-looking pants that I made you myself."

Papi turned green. He looked for something to hit her with . . . and that's where I would like to do a rewind on this movie. Understand me?

I see myself at that moment going into the fogón and taking my dad into a corner. Then I say to him: "Let's get moving right now. Let's go!" In another version, I go into the fogón and I yell: "If you don't respect your wife, then you will respect my mother!", and I punch him right in the face.

I see all that in little movies in my mind. But to tell the truth, the truth is that I did nothing. Nothing to defend my own mother! I just watched them with that acid taste in my mouth.

Then my father found a piece of *guayabo* wood and began to hit Mai in the head, her face. I could have avoided it. But no. Mai fell to the ground. The blood began to squirt out of her head. She just laid down on the floor. Then my father began to hit the walls of the *fogón* to break it all to pieces. The fogón that my brothers and I had built with so much care the year before, beginning of Christmas time. Then he saw me at the little doorway. I gave him a look like asking him: "Why?" and he took that piece of wood like he was going to hit me too. I went running. Running away from him like a dog. I didn't confront him. I didn't say a word. And then he turned and went walking down the same path he had come up on, to have his lunch at someone else's house, where he would be treated like a king.

I could have done something. I could have
stopped the blood that ran down my mom's head. I
went back to where she was, and I looked at her. I
couldn't believe what I was seeing. My father killed my
mother in front of my eyes and I did nothing. Nothing!
I said nothing. I did nothing! I felt hatred. Hatred
toward my father. I vomited next to the *fogón*. I felt
so dirty inside, I just wanted to die. I wanted to die!
Then I started running as if I was still drunk. Drunk
and desperate. I was crying. I felt like vomiting
again. I kept on running, dragging myself along from
tree to tree, until I got to doña Cesi's house.

"Cesi!, Cesi!", I yelled. "Calixto broke Mai's head
open in the fogón."

Doña Cecilia let go of her iron and picked up
her little machete. She cut some *escoba* plants and
some common plantain leaves. She picked up a jar of
something green, some bandages, needles, thread. She
took off running. I lay down there waiting for death
to take me. I didn't die. I just felt filthy and sick and
lazy. When I got back to the *fogón,* Mai's head was
all clean and bandaged up. She was unconscious but
breathing ok.

My father came home that night as if nothing
had happened. I didn't look at him. His presence
disgusted me. I wanted to yell: "Dirty animal, you
almost killed my mother!" But I didn't say anything. I
felt hatred and fear at the same time. Me! The same
guy who had felt like such a big man the night before,

drinking moonshine! I felt real small. Small and dirty. Another stupid coward. I'm a coward. That is why I detest this life. And I feel lost.

I'm not saying that what my father did is the cause of my problems, but that day I felt for the first time what I call my "condition," whatever the hell is wrong with me. First off, what I say means nothing. My words are no good and neither am I, and I'm sure the great Calixto would agree. If I say I'm going to do something, I don't do it. It even *bothers* me to say I'm going to do something. Instead of saying: "I said I was going to do this and I am betting on me," that commitment drags on me. It stinks! It puts me in a bad mood. Then there's that anxiety that doesn't let me rest, you know? And when I have to choose between doing something the right way or hurrying up and doing it any which way, I choose to hurry up and do it all wrong because I got no energy to do it any other way.

Once I went to a psychologist, but he just sat there giving me advice. That I shouldn't drink so much, that I shouldn't smoke so much weed. I never told him about the *perico*, because that is sacred to me. Nobody's going to take Blanca away from me! She's the only thing that helps me to feel good about myself. She gives me energy and more. She takes away the bad feelings I have toward myself. And when I'm all high, people love me! Everyone thinks I'm great fun!

They told me about some old people, a couple from Almácigo, the *barrio* next to Piñales, where

I grew up. One day, about ten years ago, near my birthday, I went there because somebody told me they took difficult cases, deep problems, impossible cases, you know. I was going to ask them to help me get free from the desperation I feel in my body, the anxiety, the constant questions: "What is it that's missing? Why do I always feel so anxious, as if something terrible is going to happen to me?" And "what is making me feel that I'm not even me?" That sort of thing. The old guy's name was don Hernán, I remember. The lady, I don't remember. But when I got there, the old man had just died, the old lady was in bed, and she was really, really old! That day, I felt so desperate, I don't even want to remember that day!

So then I went to see a priest, and he sent me to a psychiatrist. A famous shrink, the one who talks on television after the 5 o'clock news. He gave me some pills that make me feel like I'm in some kind of straight jacket and everything is happening someplace far away from me. And they are expensive! So I stopped going there. I didn't like that guy. He said that I was depressed. I say the day that my dad killed the love I had for him, something inside of me died too. Make sense? I'm always looking for myself, looking for my own self. And I never find me. I don't know how to deal with this. Most of the time I just feel lost. Sometimes something – or someone – shakes me up and I almost feel like me for a few seconds. But that doesn't last. I don't know how to be myself again. I only know that I'm not me. So I look for my essence in church and in cokaine, which is a great help. At least, with my *perico* I see things real clear. Got that? With four lines of *perico* I sat right down and wrote you all this little story. That's how things are! And then they tell you that drugs are bad. Unless you buy them at the drugstore, right? The ones the doctors prescribe, right? They're all good!

You can send your prayers right to me. And you can tell other people what I'm looking for to see if someone can help me.

So the "author" of this book ain't so bad after all. She let me make this big announcement here in her book, and she didn't charge me a penny.

Chapter eight

Lola's number

•

It's not easy to start a new life alone at 34 in a culture that you identify as yours but that is practically unknown to you. Lola is brave. She decided to move to her maternal family's home town and – after three days of walking the sunny streets of Mayagüez – came upon the little house that she would rent for the next seven years.

From her new abode, Lola enjoyed a spectacular view of barrio Jácanas, where dozens of houses sprouted wildly among mango, breadfruit, cashew, *corazón* and *guanábana* trees. The first time her aunts and cousins looked out from her balcony, they were speechless to see that she also had a perfect view of the place where her mother's mother and eleven great aunts and uncles had all been born in a shack made of palm wood and *yaguas* at the end of the 19th century, now occupied by a two-story cement house, freshly painted lime green with bright orange trim.

The neighbors did not understand the presence of an *americana* of her age without a husband or even children in a *barriada* where everyone was family or at the very least, a working class *mayagüezano*. The fact that she had no furniture in her rented cottage didn't help, and a misunderstood "wanted" poster, demanding freedom for Puerto Rican political prisoners, led the local gentlemen to believe that she was a narcotics agent, ready to flee after her first big raid. Lola froze

inside when one day her next-door neighbor asked to
see her official *cañón!* She raised even more suspicion
when she bought the bolitero's green jalopy for $550.
(Lola was born in 1955, so that price seemed to be
favored by the numerological gods, still unfamiliar
to her but emphatically admired.) A 30-something,
college-educated, white lady running around in Chino
Rullán's old Skylark! She just *had* to be an agent! Of
course, Lola did not use her car to hang with drug
dealers. She only went to the university and to a small
shoe repair store that served as a social center for the
independentista community. The neighbors might have
suspected her political affinities, but their version made
for juicier conversations!

Most of the ladies wanted nothing to do with her.
A shapely, laughing, *salsagorda*-loving neighbor with
no husband in sight represented a threat, especially
since her insistence in transforming a cement patio into
a garden for vegetables and aromatic plants required
wheelbarrows full of earth, agricultural consultations
and frequent truck rides from the very willing, handy
and handsome men who enjoyed her quirky company and
the wildly embellished gossip it would soon provide.

As you might imagine, Lola was eager to break
the barriers to her full integration into the culture of
Vista Limón and of her motherland. Among these, the
numbers barrier seemed to be the biggest of all.

Surrounded by enthusiastic numbers runners and
players, every single day, Lola heard about *"números*

bonitos" and "*números feos*" that arrived in dreams.
For Lola, these were strangely meaningful giants that
loomed mysteriously from neighborhood conversations.
Pretty numbers? Ugly numbers? With all of her being,
Lola tried to understand these denominations, but she
just could not get it. And so for Lola, the numbers
mystery symbolized an essence that she would have
to understand before she could fully participate in a
culture whose music, botanical culture and human
warmth she adored.

Would she ever truly become part of this new
world of her *barrio*? It was time to be proactive! So,
armed with her culinary specialties, she began visiting
the Rullans. She longed to feel part of the good *bolitero*
family. But while they were polite, a friendship did not
take hold because they simply did not trust her. Surely,
thought Lola, they distrusted her because she obviously
did not understand the most basic elements of the world
of numbers. She would have to learn to play in that key!

During those early Mayagüez nights, Lola prayed
to her deceased and very beloved grandmother Mariana
and her grandmother's sister Micaela (*espiritista*, by
the way) so that they might please illuminate her mind,
reveal to her – through an omen, a dream, perhaps –
something of the secret. Just a hint would suffice!
What could be the true meaning of the numbers? Lola
lost a lot of sleep trying to figure it all out.

Until, just about a month after receiving her long-
lost furniture from La Flor de Mayo Express Movers,

Lola enjoyed a great little dinner of fresh fish with her specialty dish of mashed *yautía* with browned onions, topped with wild nettles and marjoram. That same night, she dreamed about . . . the cat!

The three-colored cat, obviously a nursing mother, circled the freshly discarded skeletons of two yellow-tailed snapper fish. Upon finding their delicious and gummy eyes still intact, she screamed with pleasure as only a cat can, with a voice, that if the neighbors could hear her, they would stone her to death. Incredibly, Lola understood the long, hard and badly-tuned feline siren:

"MIAOWAAAAWOOOOWWWOOOOOOOW. ¡GRAAAAACIAS! ¡GRRRRAAAAAAACCIIIAAAAAS POR LA COMIIIIIIIIIIIDAAA!"

"THAAANK YOU! THAAANK YOUUUU for the FOOOOOOOD."

Within her dream, surprised by the cat's politeness and gratitude, Lola responded with a loving: "You're welcome, *mi'hijita*. Any time I eat fresh fish, you'll find the leftovers in that very same corner of the garden. *¡Que te aproveche!* May it be your medicine, baby!"

"¡PLAAAAAY, my FRIEEEEND. PLAAAAAY! The NUUUUMBEEER!"

"Play! Oh my GODDESS! Play? What number should I play?

And in an act of spiritual bilocation never before experienced and never to be repeated, Lola sat up in her bed and, lucidly participating in her dream, grabbed pen and paper while she awaited the fateful numerals of her fortune:

NUUUUUEEEEEVVVVVE

SIIIIIIEEEEEEETEEEEEEEE

DOOOOOOOOOOS.

9-7-2. 9-7-2. She wrote it down still sleeping.

Then suddenly, Lola woke up. She turned on the lights and stared without blinking, for the longest time, those digits that promised her material wellbeing, and – far more importantly – integration, participation, acceptance. *¡Comunión cultural!* Her loyal ancestors and the Boricua divinities of good fortune had finally seen fit to speak to her through the purest of messengers. Finally!

In part, because of the disorientation a prophetic dream can cause, or maybe for another unknown reason, Lola chose to play her cherished number in a public, legal venue instead of going to the Rulláns house. She got out of bed early and ran to the bakery where a new Pega-3 machine had recently been installed. While waiting for the machine to be turned on, she tried to decide if she should play all of the $13 she had for that day's expenses.

Finally, a short, plump little *doña* with white, freckly skin, a big, black bun and very thick glasses announced that she could play her three-digit number.

"*Trece pesos* on 9-7-2," said Lola, with the nervousness that exaggerated her newyorican accent.

"¿Tres pesos exacto?"

"Trece."

The woman at the register looked shocked.
Equally surprised was a tall, elegant, very dark-skinned
man buying Mallorca pastries and a 50-something,
blonde-haired socialite lady with honey-colored skin and
El Vocero in her left hand. At the bakery in barrio La
Salud, a gringa who played $13 on a Pega-3 number was
not something you saw very often. At all.

In the midst of the silence, Lola received
her tickets and offered her last bills to the *doña* at
the register. As she left, she heard her number in
masculine and feminine voices. Her intuition told her
that this could be a bad sign. She said a quick prayer
that their interest would not be unlucky for her, and
left the situation in the hands of her totally miraculous
destiny.

That day, there was no money for lunch, but Lola
didn't care. Her euphoric certainty of becoming – so
very soon – a big-time winner, suppressed the most basic
instinct of all living creatures. She made the supreme
sacrifice and contained herself, saying nothing about
the wonderful dream to her work-mates. At 4:30 she
flew from her office anxious to receive the good news
in a clean and orderly space. At 10 pm, Lola had even
cleaned the innards of her refrigerator, for her nerves
had lent her unmatched vigor in the hygiene department.
She was sitting on the edge of the hammock when they
finally announced:

NUEVE. Inhale. Exhale. Inhale.

SIETE. Exhale. Inhale. Exhale.

OCHO.

¿Nueve siete ocho? Nine seven eight? Eight? Impossible! This is impossible? How is it possible that the cat could trick her this way? Betrayed by a thankful cat? That can't be! Nine seven eight? Impossible!

Lola lost sleep *that* night trying to understand the inexplicable, the incomprehensible. She could not shut her eyes. The next day, before going off to work, she took a delicious cornmeal-coconut breakfast to Paula Vargas, her closest and most trusted neighbor.

"You have to keep playing it," Paula explained with patience and good humor. "Or . . . maybe that number is not for you!"

"How's that?"

"Sometimes, you get a number for another person. For example, you give me that number, I play it, and I win. Well, that number was for me!"

"I get it," said Lola, without getting it at all.

After a long silence, she armed herself with courage to ask the question that would forever brand her as a foreigner: "*Oye*, Paula. ¿What do you think? Is 9-7-2 a pretty number?"

"Pretty it's not, but don't you worry. This Thursday, I'll play it and we'll see what happens. If I win something, I'll give you a tip. Now do you get it?"

"I receive a number. I give it to you. You play it. You win. And you give *me* a tip." Lola's head was reeling with this cultural treasure trove, this numerological dimension to her newly acquired mercurial vocation. Fascinating! Fantastic!

That day, Lola headed off for work with sweaty hands and a mixed-up mind. If the number was not for her, ¿why had she received it from a grateful cat? If the cat was so thankful, ¿why in the Goddess's name didn't she give her a "pretty" number? If numbers are innocent symbols, how is it possible that there be "ugly" numbers?

She also asked herself if perhaps her brain, blocked from childhood with relation to mathematics, simply was not registering something that for the rest of the world was clear and elemental. She could not concentrate on her questionnaire work nor even on Carlos Quintana's funny stories; Carlos, who always helped her feel closer to the culture she so desired to be part of. It was total obsession. However, the next day, Lola felt somewhat recuperated and almost initiated, eager to follow Paula's good advice.

She kept on playing, each time with less money and in a different place. She even played the *bolita dominicana!* At the same time, she visited every single one of her neighbors. Lola entered their homes like a missionary of the faith to share the mysterious tale and make the offering of her number. Within two months, she had told the cat story to dozens of people,

including the *boliteros*, the gossip lovers of Vista
Limón, her mechanic – to whom she owed more than
$70 – those who ate lunch with her at doña Aurea's
fonda, and all of her buddies at work. Wherever Lola
walked, people yelled out: "*¡Oye!* Dreamed of any cats
lately?" Question followed by ironic smiles and laughter.
And it didn't bother her in the least. On the contrary!
That was just the kind of question one would ask the
daughter of a numbers runner. An inside, community
joke! More than 60 years after her grandparents moved
from Mayagüez never to return, Lola had become a joke
in their very same ancestral community.

•

Two months after that dream, at about seven in
the evening, Lola was mopping the floor when a three-
colored cat sauntered into her home. She watched as
the cat slinked around the periphery of the entire house,
and left just as she had entered. A laughing Lola
pretended to chase her with a broom: "Get out of here,
you little traitor, you!"

Three hours later, she heard yelling in the street.
She rushed out of her shower to find herself facing
a brigade of neighbors all anxious to know if she
had played her famous number. "The cat's number
won tonight!" about ten people screamed as a chorus.
"*Nueve-siete-dos* won the Pega-3!"

That very next Saturday, Lola found herself
buying supplies at the neighborhood market. Fragrant

of indigo soap and *galletas María,* the *Colmado Colom's* aisles were so narrow you had to walk sideways like a crab to avoid knocking down the contents of the shelves. So it was a little strange to see her mechanic, the corpulent Ramón Rosado, avidly pursuing her.

"Lola! . . . Lolín!", he shouted, animatedly gesticulating with his muscular arms. Lola smiled as she waved hi, but Ramón insisted, now daring to walk with his big swing through the home products aisle, knocking down a stack of toilet paper rolls, sponges and little boxes of Brillo. Watching this excessive show of affection, Lola understood that he had been drinking. In order to avoid more destructive cascades, she walked quickly over to him right between the votive candles, the cotton mops and an avalanche of Vel. Ramón grabbed her, and with his great, working man's hug, he yelled for all to hear: "I won with the cat's number, Lola! I won with the cat! So you don't owe me nothing! You don't owe me one cent, Lola!

And then, an unreal, much-too-loud echo surrounded her:

"He won with the cat's number!

"Ramón won with the cat!"

"No kidding!"

"Really?"

"No kidding, man. Of course! With 9-7-2!

"Lola's number!"

The message was heard dozens of times. Her
number was repeated among the twenty-or-so people
in the *colmado*, all witnesses to the cancellation of her
debt. "And the alternator. The alternator is gonna be
free for you!", called out the overalled Ramón. "I won
BIG TIME!"

•

At the moment of the hug and the echo, Lola
also won with the cat's number. At that very instant,
she crossed through the portal that opens only to the
initiated, those who belong, our people, *nuestra gente*.
Never to turn back.

And as far as the numbers go, well suddenly,
there was nothing else to understand. In spite of
other peoples' opinions to the contrary, 9-7-2 is a most
beautiful number, indeed. Of that, Lola is more than
certain, and no-one will ever convince her otherwise.

Chapter nine

Poison

•

During the 1970s, Lola lived in New York's Catskill Mountains among independent, spiritual eco-feminists. They built their own homes and explored the worlds of solar energy, high-efficiency wood stoves, organic farming, animal husbandry, medical self-sufficiency, drum circles, dances to the Great Mother and rites of love for Gaia. Under the elders' guidance, Lola hammered roofs, killed chickens for their soups, repaired shoes, harvested medicinal herbs, planted vegetables, prepared botanical oils and gave lots of therapeutic massage. She also slept under the trees, swam naked in lakes, ponds and rivers, and in countless other ways celebrated her liberation from the rote, established pattern of marriage and children. Lola chose instead to cultivate herself by writing, dancing and drumming under every lunar phase. She filled her lungs with the smoke of natural resins and leaves, always experimenting with new ways of seeing, new ways of living.

Yoko "the hippy" lived in a parallel world in Puerto Rico. This thin Taíno-type, with his long black mane and strong convictions, got together with the beautiful, Afro-Rican Anabela, and together they threw to one side the comforts and social benefits of urban life. Thanks to countless personal sacrifices, loans and promises, they were able to buy several acres of land on the east coast of Borinken, just above the coral reefs in a coastal forest of cliffs and vines. There, they struggled to make their agricultural dream come true. Little by little, they became part of the rural community of barrio Marimbo . . . although in spite of many conversations and years of being neighbors, the locals preferred never to call them by their names. They were always simply "the hippies."

•

A friend in New York connected Lola with Yoko and Anabela during her first visit to Borinquen, while doing a cultural study. Lola was learning from the herbalists and bone setters, the midwives and the farmers who could teach her about the island's ancestral healing traditions. She arrived at Yoko's and Anabela's farm following a magical three-day visit with *abuela* Eugenia Quiñones Pérez, whose deeply-rooted wisdom and knowledge imprinted upon Lola the inseparable relationships between nature and healing; devotion and miracles.

Inspired and feeling deeply honored, Lola arrived at the hippies' territory anxious to work on the farm and thus contribute to the family's way of life. That land supplied them with root vegetables, leaves, fruits and flowers, which the visionary couple sold in the city to a new generation that appreciated the true value of food cultivated without synthetic chemicals, the *abuelos'* way.

Yoko explained tirelessly to his urban friends how the Puerto Rican people had been taught to disdain their rural culture and to abandon the very practices that would guarantee the sustainable autonomy that so many of them aspired to. Yoko explained how their colonizers had done the unspeakable to erase the roots of Puerto Rican identity and, at the same time, promote the type of economic progress that would guarantee a comfortable, submissive "territory," spiritually incapable of creating a dignified, sovereign future.

Lola understood Yoko's reasons. Besides, they both deeply loved nature, and shared the ideal of cultural conservation rooted in the country's most venerable agricultural and botanical traditions.

Yoko aspired to being a healer and he proclaimed himself a radical feminist; so it didn't seem too strange when he asked Lola all about her "female cycles" and about her erotic and reproductive experiences. Her friendship with Yoko was one of philosophical complicity, and she greatly admired his commitment to the hard physical work needed to maintain their farm of ocean views and healthful harvests. Even so, the ideological rigidity of this man and his need to always have the first and last word provoked in her a sense of sadness for the obvious character imbalances that she did not know how to treat.

Lola loved Anabela and her daughters with a passion, and she sang, danced and dramatized with them at every opportunity in their wooden house between the forest and the sea. That feminine, intergenerational connection was the most important part for Lola.

During her first visits of play, volunteer work
and philosophical exchange, she started visualizing
a move from her beloved New York. Thanks to her
experiences with Anabela's family, she understood that
in Borinquen she would find true friends, people who
would understand her in spite of the cultural norms
that grossly misunderstood her expressions of feminine
freedom. For Lola, the physical distance between
Marimbo and New York hardly mattered because she
and her pioneering friends were deeply united by their
values and their Gaia-centered world view.

•

After her move to Vista Limón, just one week
after buying her neighbor Rullán's old, green Skylark,
Lola made the nine-hour pilgrimage on the Panoramic
route from the opposite coast to visit Yoko and Bela.
Besides her physical work on the farm, walks, dances
and stories with the girls, and creative explorations
of beaches, rivers and farmlands, Lola invested long
nocturnal hours in prayerful silence, thankful for her
stay in that wild space that populated her dreams with
ancestral visions and messages. From the balcony that
was her guest room, under velvet black skies dressed
with infinite stars, Lola slept blessed by the lightning
bugs and inexplicably comforted by the holy racket of
countless *coquíes,* owls, waves and wind.

Several months later, almost a year after her move
to Vista Limón, Lola got a university job. The only thing
missing was full acceptance by the people in her *barriada*

when – early one Sunday morning – her friend from
barrio Marimbo paid her a surprise visit. On one hand,
she was happy to see her copper-colored friend. But his
outrageous clothing was a bit shocking, and she felt a bit
uncomfortable with the idea that he might want to spend
the night. In that community, where absolutely everything
the *americana* did was big news, it did not bode well that
another man might stay over. Two weeks before, Lola had
received a visit from her ex-*compañero* from New York,
whose humble family in Ponce had lent him a car to see
how things were going for her in Borinquen. Day after
day, Lola received a torrent of comments and questions
about the visit of her "little boyfriend."

And now Yoko! Long and skinny as a tapeworm,
bearded like Melchior and crowned by a black mane that
reached his thighs, the scantily-clad hippy decided to
practice his long chant and yogi-dance in the street in
front of Lola's home while the innocent one prepared
a lunch to meet the needs of two, hefty day laborers.
The gossip began to run its course after the thin man's
first "full-body twist with gentle-warrior cry for life"
before the astonished gaze of entire families who
distractedly drank black coffee or freshly squeezed
juice from the grapefruits of their patios. By the time
Yoko had finished his complex "resounding-movement-
excess-chi salute to the sun, with floating reverence to
the invisible moon," the residents of the entire *barriada*
were enjoying coconut water with rum on the stairways
and hammocks of the houses closest to Lola's so as not
to miss even one tiny detail of the unusual scene.

Soon, Lola began to hear the hearty laughter that was by now a familiar warning. Once again, helpless to make it right, the *americana* had committed yet another memorable cultural error.

That night, Yoko offered her a foot massage, and Lola happily accepted. At least that would help her to neutralize some of the tension his visit was causing. After the reflexological massage that came plagued by questions about her medical intimacies, Yoko looked at her intensely and said: "Lola, I've come here to invite you to be a part of our family and live in the little wooden house just above ours. I'm planning to fix it up real nice for you."

Surprised, Lola answered: "Why, thank you for the invitation, my friend. Thank you for thinking of me with so much love and trust. Wow! I am so honored .... But I am happy *here.* After living my whole life in New York, I'm finally learning and participating in a social life in my *barrio.* I love my job at the University, and it offers me ways to be part of our country's culture. Every day!"

"You don't understand me, Lola. I've been observing you on the farm. I've seen you work and I know that you were not born to be sitting in an office without windows. You love the farm . . . and I need you. *We* need you. I'm offering you an opportunity to be part of a movement, the most important movement of our times! And it's not so you can live on the farm alone! I'm inviting you to be my woman. My second

130

woman. I want you to give me sons, Lola. Sons to work with me on the farm!"

Had she heard right? His second woman? Give him sons? Lola had never wanted to be a mother. The last thing she wanted was to birth the sons of a guy who didn't love her and that she didn't love. What on earth was this boy smoking?

"And Anabela wants me there as your second wife?"

Silence.

"Bela just told me not to wreck our friendship with you."

Lola was even more uncomfortable now. All this about giving him sons without being in love, without any kind of feeling. As if he were asking for a simple favor, like maybe taking him to the airport in Isla Verde! But when a machista guy is sharing your little house at 11 pm, you don't bother him with arguments or insults, or even clear feminist reasoning. Lola kept her thoughts to herself so she could rest and not polarize the issue. "There's no way that your invitation could wreck our friendship, Yoko. I'm sorry, but it's just not a good moment for me. I have finally arrived! I've come home to the town of my maternal ancestors . . . and I love Mayagüez. I love my new job! I am also very honored that you have thought about me in such a loving way. *¡Gracias!*

Now she felt a little better. Surely, Yoko did not understand what he was asking because he didn't know

her too well. Maybe he thought she was dying to be
a mother! If he knew what Lola wanted to create in
Borinquen, he would not ask this of her. Right? But wait
a minute! What about those long conversations they'd
had about Lola's visions and goals? It hurt to think that
her friend had not really listened to her at all.

While those thoughts flew around her mind, Lola
struggled to calm herself. She said a very neutral
"buenas noches" after making a great little nest for
her friend on the floor. Disconcerted, she lay down
on her little bed (too narrow for sharing, thank the
Goddess!). From the bedroom doorway, Yoko kept trying
to convince her.

"Lola, I know that you love our farm. Think
about your own health! Your well being! Think about
that! Our beautiful air, our land, our sun, our own
little beach! The trees, Lola. The plants! Think about
that. And what about giving your body a chance to
live its femininity? Your body is begging you for the
experience of being a complete woman. You *need* to be
a mother! And what could be better for all of us than
your being the mother of my sons?"

Mother of his sons? What planet has he been
hanging at? Lola wondered. But she said: "Look, my
friend. I care about you a lot, and you know how much
I love your family. But try to understand me. I'm
saying no. Come on now. I need to sleep. Tomorrow I
get up at the crack of dawn and I need to be rested for
work."

"Think about it, Lola. Think hard about this. This is an opportunity to put into practice the ideals you *say* you share with us. These opportunities only come around once in a lifetime. They don't come but once!"

Earlier than usual, after a long, surreal night, adorned by strange sounds from Yoko's bed, Lola nearly flew from her home with more enthusiasm than ever for her work at the Colegio.

"Ay, bendito! What a girl's got to pay nowadays for a foot massage," she thought with an ironic smille as she returned to her home at 5 pm, relieved to see that her guest's van was no longer parked in front of her little home. As agreed, Yoko had left her key in an invisible, yet accessible place. Lola entered anxious to stretch and dance to the rhythm of her rumba, and reestablish her good home vibrations. But when she went to turn on the tape player, there was a piece of paper folded up where the cassette was to be played. Intrigued, she eagerly unfolded the paper. It said: "You have scorned the love of an entire family. You'll be sorry!"

The threatening tone of the note was a bit shocking, but Lola insisted on being positive. "He really is nuts!", she murmured, thankful he was gone, and that he lived far away from her west coast home.

She stretched and danced until she had worked up a good sweat. Feeling more herself, she hungrily opened her refrigerator and found yet another note in yellow paper on top of her miso soup with vegetables. "You reject the love of your unborn son."

What is this guy talking about? Unborn *son?*
Unborn son!"

Her refrigerator had become an accomplice of this
strange man! Lola began to feel invaded, judged and
mistreated, alone in her home.

By bedtime, she had found nine notes, all similar
in tone. In her underwear drawer, in the book she was
reading, in the medicine cabinet, in her jewelry box. The
last note, folded and left under her pillow, accused her of
having lost the chance to feel "thirteen orgasms a night,
in night-after-night of unforgettable ecstasy." Thirteen
orgasms a night with Yoko? That was the last straw.

After three hours of restlessness as she procured
the sweet sleep of the innocent, she got out of bed
beyond angry with her disrespectful ex-friend. She sat
down then, and wrote a furious letter. Furious and far
too honest. Upon remembering his constant "innocent"
questions about her feminine biology, green bile nearly
reached her mouth. She told that skinny malink that
she had *never* felt any kind of attraction toward him
and that now she understood that he was just another
manipulative, machista. She kept writing. The words
jumped from her mind to her daring hand in a storm of
righteous indignation.

Of course, she should have held on to that letter
so she could consider its possible effects on a masculine
ego. But her fury at feeling so fooled by a man who had
received from her such an innocently loving friendship,
pushed her to break with him once and for all. With

friends like Yoko, she preferred a clearly-identifiable enemy. With time, she thought, she would find a way to reestablish her connection with Anabela and the girls.

Innocent indeed, Lola could not imagine the malice of this so-called revolutionary with a hunger for polygamy.

•

Years later, she came across Anabela at a mountain music festival. Lola went running toward her friend, smiling and eager. Surprisingly, without even giving Lola a look in the eye, Anabela made a sharp NO gesture, crossing her open hand in front of Lola's face in a horizontal line. Lola didn't understand and looked for her friend's familiar smile. "Bela, it's me. Lola!" But Anabela kept walking, moving quickly away amidst the crowd, protecting the girls from Lola's unbelieving gaze.

Some fifteen years after Lola's strange encounter with Yoko, after having been mysteriously rejected several times by Anabela, her daughters and other young people that Lola identified as her tribe, she discovered that out of revenge, the man had defamed her for years, spreading the rumor that Lola was a federal agent. An undercover cop! Spy! Informer! Stool pigeon! Mole! FBI! CIA!

On the Puerto Rican archipelago, undercover agents of the FBI and and other such organizations have conspired for over a century to spy, jail, torture and kill hundreds of leaders identified with the ideal of Puerto Rico's independence and political sovereignty. The presence of those agents in this colonized nation is a living venom that silences, threatens and paralyzes through fear, suspicion, division and betrayal. Imagine the mentality of someone who accuses a woman of being an undercover spy to get back at her for an offense to his masculine ego. Absurd, cruel, dangerous, insane!

•

Lola now understands that innocence must be tempered with great wisdom, and that sleepless anger is a poor counselor at the moment of writing a letter. Even so, reflecting upon her act, she is not sorry she shut that door good and shut . . . and forever.

Chapter 10

Return. Retrieve.

•

From her bed, Eugenia radiated peace. "When you're born with the gift, whatever happens, that gift will always be with you, Valeria. Most people don't understand. Making peace with your gift is solitary work. And it takes time. But little by little you get to know yourself and you come to a better understanding of that seeing, that knowing. You have a divine talent that will allow you to help those most in need. You will be a light in the darkness . . . . You cry now, mi *hija*. You cry, and I understand. But when you graduate from college, you will take my place here in Almácigo. And from above, beloved, I will help you as well as I can. Now, my daughter, you must get going. They'll be here any moment to pick you up. We both know it's for the greatest good."

Encircled by the pale pink veil of Geña's mosquito netting, Valeria treasured that last moment before her teacher, her mentor, the person who best understood her. But she also felt the pain of what felt like too much emotion: enormous sadness before their imminent separation, fear, and confidence all at once.

Valeria was comfortable with her abilities, and she followed her intuition with integrity. She also trusted in the recurring dreams both Geña and she'd had about her destiny and the need for her to go and know the world on the other side of the ocean, the world of those who

had left the island. But take the place of her teacher
when she returned? How could she do that *and* earn a
living?

She thought about her older sister who got a kick
out of ridiculing her. *"Curandera?* Haven't you noticed
that now we have modern hospitals? You must be out
of your mind! Or maybe you want to follow in Maí's
footsteps, dying without a penny to her name? What
are you going to charge for your services? A dollar for
your candles? A ball of cheese? No, no. I know!", she
laughed sarcastically: "a farm hand to plant your yams!
Ha! Get with it, sister!"

Everyone told her that as soon as she got to New
York City, she would forget about "all that" and move on
to better her life. But Valeria was clear.

•

Geña had adopted "Vale" when she was 11 years
old, just after the death of her mom, Mai Ceci. Cecilia
had offered 20 years of service as her *barrio's* midwife,
a service which, in the sixties, began to embarrass her
urban relatives.

When the time came to find homes for the good
midwife's children, her eldest daughter cried to be
released from the "jungle" and went to live with cousins
in the Bronx who would show her the *good* life. But
Valeria had another idea. Her mother's work had always
moved her heart. She enjoyed the intimate service
among neighbors, and she adored the smells, views,

sounds and flavors of her land, of her barrio Piñales. The girl begged her great uncle Carmelo until one day, he finally relented and took her to the next *barrio* to visit doña Eugenia and don Hernán, the last *curanderos* of Almácigo.

When they arrived, Valeria surprised everyone with her proposal of exchanging domestic work for bed and board. She showed great interest in learning from her elderly neighbors. Doña Geña had come to her rescue more than once when the legendary abdominal *empachos* of her childhood could only be cured by the healing rubs and teas offered by the beautiful old lady whose hands smelled slightly of burnt coconut oil.

They made a provisional arrangement, but from that very first day, the presence of the bright and helpful youngster comforted Geña's heart. She was relieved to know that her knowledge would finally be passed on to someone with the compassion and sense of justice that would honor their practice. Nan was also delighted to have someone to teach about the animals, herbs, bushes and trees that had been his university.

Valeria knew that she had been well adopted and loved. But at the end of the 20th century, how in the world could she possibly comply with a job as big as following in Geña's footsteps?

"*Mi hija*, remember your gratitudes, your offerings. Give thanks always to our Blessed Mother of Miracles who lives within your heart and mine; the Great Mother who inhabits all of our Earth, and all the plants and

animals we eat, who is present in your perfect body, in
every drop of your sweat, in your restful nights. Thank
the Great Holy Spirit who gives life to every drop of
rain that falls, to the air we breathe in the infinite sky,
to every ray of sunlight, to every drop of our medicines."

Suddenly, Geña looked at her with a soft smile. "I
don't know what New York is like, but if you can't make
your offerings like we do here, don't worry. Before I
got together with Nan, I made them differently myself.
Listen up now. If I was dancing and enjoying my good
health, I simply dedicated my dance to the healing
of someone who was sick. If I was going through a
difficult passage, any trial of life, I dedicated my
sacrifice and my strength to the people who were
most needy of that strength. There are so many
ways of making offerings! There are so many ways to
pray, aren't there? And they are all part of your gift.
Because you have always understood about offerings
and gratitudes, my daughter."

Geña was silent for a few seconds, and they heard
a taxi pulling up to wait for Valeria.

"I'm proud of you, my girl. Remember I will
always be there for you, here in Almácigo and wherever
you may roam. Now and from heaven above. You can
always count on me!"

With cheeks wet from her tears, Valeria pressed
her lips lightly to her teacher's forehead and smelled for
the last time her aroma of bricks warmed by the sun's
rays. As always, her white hair and her saintly hands

smelled of coconut oil that had been ever-so-lightly singed by the fire.

Then, holding back an explosion of anguish, the young lady slipped out from under the mosquito netting and walked with her suitcase toward the future.

•

After more than 30 years of study and intense experiences in New York, Valeria was finally on her way home to claim her place in the lineage of spiritual service that her teachers had prepared her for. Her first years in the big city had been unimaginably challenging. That first "bilingual" semester at the university took her to the edge of collapse. Then, almost miraculously, she found the Centro Cultural del Barrio and a group of theatre people, dancers, singers and percussionists who initiated her in the worlds of romance, urban gardens and dozens of cultural and academic reasons to honor her memories, her passions and her secret goals. Finally, recently freed of an exhausting sentimental relationship, she was returning with a doctorate degree in psychology, several clients and students she saw regularly by Skype, and a university salary as long-distance mentor, professor and counselor.

In spite of the pact Valeria had made to return to barrio Almácigo, it was her native Piñales that welcomed her when she returned from New York. Because Almácigo had been converted into a series of gated communities with names like Almácigo Breezes and Wild Palm Estates. There were few *almácigo* trees left, and the only palms around were the exotic "ornamental" ones planted – one in front of each house – within a desert of cement, asphalt and enormous media antennas carefully set up to receive entertaining propaganda. Most young residents used the name of their community without knowing that the *almácigo* trees had sustained entire families in times of famine and that their resin had healed and illuminated generations of their ancestors.

•

Valeria lit her candles. The first one was dedicated to the Blessed Mother of Miracles; another one to the Great Spirit; and the third – before her most treasured photographs – to her spiritual family: Cecilia, her mother, proudly donning her midwife apron; Hernán Osorio Cosme harvesting sesame with gusto at 88 years old; Eugenia Quiñones Pérez at 92 with her long braids tied up in a bun, *café* con *leche*-colored skin and a provocative shine in her joyful, ever-youthful eyes.

She bowed her head before lighting the fourth candle to the Christ of Healing, custodian of the soul of her client Manuel Milagros, a man with a great heart, who had let himself be dragged away from his essence; first by pain, and later by euphoria.

Valeria closed her eyes to remember her last conversation with Geña so many years before. "You are with me here now, my teacher. I ask for your presence among the Great Spirit, Healing Christ and our Sacred

Mother of Miracles, Mother of God. May my work be
holy, may my work be blessed. Bless me, Mamá Geña!"

As she finished her prayers, two, sixty-something,
firm-handed men knocked on the door. Dino,
percussionist and craftsman, embraced a drum he had
built of *guaraguao* wood, our native mahogany, topped
by a newly-cured goat skin. Manuel Milagros, known
as Mago, held under his arm a man-size, palm-leaf
mat he had woven the week before. It was his third
visit. After receiving an orientation and beginning
his healing process, today he would experience the
retrieval.

Dino was there in representation of their barrio
Piñales, the community that had witnessed the birth and
growth of Mago. Dino's fraternal love, his willingness
to accompany his friend and drum for him were
palancas or levers of support that would help Mago to
find and incorporate the spirit that had abandoned him.

They were received by Lola, student of the
plants and healing traditions of their nation. She
had discovered doña Geña during her first visit to
the archipelago. A year later, she found Valeria in
New York, studying psychology at the same university
where Lola studied anthropology. Their friendship
was nourished and enriched by dozens of creative
collaborations.

Dino, Mago and Lola walked to the back yard,
designed to honor Geña and Nan. Just as in the *abuelos'*
own healing space, the pummeled-earth floor of the

batey was swept to a shine. About 30 meters from the road, two walls made of long, native logs covered with vines hid their space from the passing world. They were clearly in the territory of Osain, divinity of the forest and wild healing plants.

There was one simple chair, a small altar with its photographs and candles . . . and on the floor, another, smaller rustic mat made from *yarey* palm leaves. Valeria was waiting for them there. Dino, Lola and Vale were a small community of support that would push along and help to channel the deep shamanic work to be done for Mago.

After brief words of greeting and organization, Dino lifted his drum and Valeria guided all three toward the altar. They were silent while drinking Lola's tea. She had prepared it with love and gratitude from the common, mostly ignored, sacred plants of Piñales. They too were satisfied to participate once again in a ceremony of healing.

The smell of fresh palm fibers soon gave way to the aroma of *almácigo's* purifying resin. Mago remained standing before an image of Christ the Healer and a *cemí* carved in native cedarwood with the face and hands of the Mother of Miracles. Dino sat in the chair and placed the rustic drum between his knees. He began playing an ancestral rhythm they had chosen as a group.

Lola held nine boughs of *santa maría*, a bush which – thanks to their old Cuban neighbor Joaquín

Pinares – was still known in some parts of Piñales by
its Cuban name: *rompezaragüey. Rompezaragüey* had
worked its medicine for centuries thanks to the good
communication and joining of wills between the plants
and their peoples. Lola wet the leaves in freshly blessed
rain water and asked that their pure, cleansing spirit
do its miraculous work of breaking with the past. Then
she brushed the plant's aromatic branches over the face,
head, shoulders, chest, back, lower torso, legs and feet of
Manuel Milagros.

Meanwhile, Valeria passed the smoke of *almácigo*
resin around Dino and his drum. She then offered
Mago a smudge accompanied by her song. She had
received the melody in a dream about her teachers Geña
and Nan. Lola and Dino sang with her: Dino with his
deep voice, and Lola with her improvised harmonies.
The sound danced through the thick *almácigo* smoke.
And when the resin had cleansed the lungs of each one,
Valeria lit a cigar rolled from the legendary tobacco of
Piñales. She exhaled the aromatic smoke with thanks
to the Taíno ancestors and to Atabeira, the Miraculous
Mother of Burenken's life cycle, carved in wood upon
the altar. She exhaled her gratitude to Osaín and all of
the African ancestors whose knowledge of plants and
prayer had offered so much to her own lineage. She
exhaled her gratitude to the *abuelos jíbaros:* farmers
and healers who represented the essence and future of a
strengthened, health-filled and upright people.

Mago lay down upon his aromatic, green, woven
mat before the altar.

Valeria was about five years old when she first
heard about this man and his courageous mother. She
knew that the birth of Abelarda's sixth child had
transformed the life of her own mother, Cecilia. Thanks
to that transformation, Valeria had the privilege
of observing and assisting local births from early
childhood. Her own destiny was indebted to the birth of
Mago, Manuel Milagros, the same man who had arrived
for his healing ceremony. For Valeria, the Mystery that
united all of them in her new healing space was simply
miraculous. She felt deeply thankful for the privilege
of participating so intimately in the life of Mago, born
standing to change the destiny of her life and that of
Mai Ceci.

She took a last sip of her brew, closed her eyes
and waited for the ancient rhythm to help her fly above
the warm, circling smoke. Soon she would be able
to see clearly how the spirit of her client had gotten
sidetracked and splintered.

Valeria placed her woven mat next to Mago's and
she lay down, ready to fly to the refuge for lost souls,
a slippery place, infinitely dangerous for anyone who
lacked protection or integrity. Valeria felt protected by
the healing spirit that worked through her. She felt the
living presence of her *cemí* and the tobacco spirit. She
saw herself surrounded by the light emanating from the
hands of our Great Mother. Finally, she perceived the
holy aromas of clean bricks under the sun's heat, and of
coconut oil, singed ever so slightly over burning coals.

Then she felt guided and strong enough to follow Mago's path. First, she was shown the way of greed, the greed that fattens in the stagnant waters of fear. The greed of winning without caring about the consequences, about the lives of others. She saw what had been destroyed: *Mago was five years old, sitting with his family in the tobacco ranch. A small stove was lit to keep them all warm and dry. Calixto carefully guided his son's hands so that for the first time, Mago might sew his bunch of tobacco leaves, a vital resource for all. There was a deep sense of wellbeing among the family members, all joined to work their vocation at those early morning hours. Dozens of roosters were crowing, and the green, aromatic leaves whispered softly as they moved through so many hands. From the fogón, Abelarda stirred their cornmeal breakfast slowly with a hand-made wooden spoon.*

Then Valeria walked the pathway of displacement and disconnection from the land, from farming. She watched carefully what had been devastated forever: *Mago was ten years old, taking the oxen to drink as his father had taught him: "Look, my son. We have to treat those oxen well. Before we eat, we take them to the river to cool down. These are noble animals,* mi hijo. *If they don't rest, if we don't take care of them, they die in the field, yoked together, giving all they've got to their labor."*

Valeria walked by the open grave of the knowledge inherited by so many generations. There she witnessed the tragic loss of the outcome of so many dialogues

between the Boricua ancestors and the animals
and plants, the rocks and the waters, the earth they
cultivated, their cooking fires and sun and stars. She
felt in her body the enormous hole made by the loss of
so much of that wisdom. The wisdom that guides the
healthy development of a people. And she observed
what had been abandoned: *Auntie Rafaela with her eyes
closed and a bunch of herbs held to her heart before
taking an aromatic bath with healing plants. Abuela
Pichi offering her gratitude before lighting the fire.
Abuelo Beto blessing himself before drawing water from
the well. The kids of Charco Prieto, all lying down at
night looking up toward the stars; their backs against
the rocks, surrounded by the sounds of the waters, and
intent upon their own contemplation of infinity with
emotions of longing, respectful surprise and belonging
. . . to the Miracle.*

She walked the path of separation between the
people and their soil, their plants, their insects and
frogs and mushrooms and birds. She saw what was
now extinct: *Mago was 12 years old, fishing during new
moon time with his dad and older brothers, equipped
only with knowledge, a sack made from maguey fibers,
and two rustic lanterns,. They were going after the fresh
water crabs that had fed so many generations of Taínos,
Jíbaros and escaped African slaves.*

Then she heard the silenced collective scream of
Mago and his family the day of the great loss. The day
the owner of their farm announced to them "the end of

tobacco, the end of farming." What would they make
of their lives? *Mago, that night, listening to the far
away voices of his uncle Daniel and his father Calixto
expressing rare emotions. Soon, the young man would
understand that the vocation he was learning with so
much joy and enthusiasm had no value in the new world
of dependence and overconsumption.*

Valeria walked through the saintly and justified
anger of the sacred plants, abused and enslaved by
human beings hungry for pleasure and freedom.

*Suddenly, Mago appeared at around 14 with his
hands tied, his heart enraged and confused. Mago
hating himself, hating his father, feeling sullied and
cowardly. At that moment, the innocence of his being
moved away from his soul. Fleeing the blood that flowed
onto the earthen floor of his family's hearth, their* fogón.

That was how Valeria observed the devastation
and the ruins, one by one: the innocence and the dreams
that had abandoned Mago and how this had happened
little by little.

●

Valeria called out to Manuel Milagros. But
instead of his name, what came out of her mouth was a
long song that described visions of two different lives:
the life he was living, and the life he could live. Lola
found phrases to repeat, and Dino answered the song's
journey with his voice and his drum. Suddenly, Dino
felt himself surrounded by stones and trees, palms and
wild fruit. He knew he was accompanied by the ancient

spirit of the forest. Osaín was present. And Dino's voice was strengthened.

Valeria observed and called out to Mago once and again with the song of contrasts: of hellish sufferings and exaggerated pleasures. And then, she sang of a life more in line with his birth and his own divine purpose.

Valeria gave a signal and the communal song came to an end. Then she called all of the Magos through another song that came to life before their eyes like a movie, starting with the day of the *corazones* by Abelarda's cabin. That song took its time.

Then Valeria asked all the past Magos and the Mago who was present if they were ready, if they were prepared, if they recognized one another, if they would be united once more, if they would commit to the retrieval.

It was Lola then who intoned the sacred song of forgiveness: the song so few of us remember and yet we all so easily recognize. Her song was gentle but with an edge just sharp enough to cut the knots and the defenses. She sang to free and cut away, to cut away and dissolve the suit of armor that kept Mago's heart separated from his vulnerable innocence. While she sang, Lola herself forgave those who had most hurt her. Nothing existed for her except forgiveness. And her song was empowered.

When Mago began to whisper from his palm mat, his words were of forgiveness for himself. He forgave himself for wanting to be someone else. He forgave

himself for his self hatred. He forgave himself for
feeling impotent, for shrinking, for looking down on his
jíbaro past, for abandoning the care of his soul. He
forgave himself with all the love he could bring together
at that moment. He rolled around and grabbed onto
his tightly woven mat. He cried with his whole body
and with a voice that surrendered more and more to
his raw emotion. Then Manuel Milagros felt, in body
and soul, the presence of his protections. That helped
him to see that he had only to open himself fully to the
Mystery and to the power of the wild, natural world, to
the Christic love that was everywhere he went, to the
Miracle of his very own being.

Lola, Valeria and Dino kept on singing while
Mago emptied himself in his cleansing and then while
he filled himself with his own power. Then the drum
sped up and suddenly they all sat there staring at one
another as if they had just woken up from an impossible
dream, a miracle shared by all four of them.

Dino took up the drum with a soothing *bomba*
rhythm, a *yubá masón*. Valeria saw Nan's eyes, Geña's
eyes, watching her thankfully. At that moment, she
understood that every forgiveness liberates those who
have lived before us; that our ancestors thankfully
receive the light that our own healing brings them.

•

When he allowed himself to feel totally bathed and
blanketed in fraternal love, Mago knew that his prayers
had been answered. He felt the most piercing, painful

sadness and grief, the recognition of terrible losses and frightening challenges ahead. Yet, in the deepest part of his body, there was a space of acceptance and welcome so big that it melted the ever-present anxiety that for so many years had driven him to avoid his own genuine and sacred emotions.

Then his impatience melted away. The desire to erase all of his pain and be totally healed after one ceremony, one retrieval, seemed to simply evaporate!

At that moment – in the presence of a soft light that emanated from the Great Atabeira of Miracles – Lola, Dino, Valeria and Mago were thankful that the truth was different. They understood that they had all participated . . . not in an ending, but a beginning. A beginning that had everything to do with the retrieval of innocence and with deep bonds of solidarity and mutual support, where the Great Mystery is at once witness and source.

Then, upon the deep-green palm leaves and clay-colored floor, their tears fell like so many of the pathways that lead us toward our true home. And Mago, receiving them as the most sacred, baptismal holy water, could only repeat, as in a dream of churches made of hanging vines, bamboos, trees and friendship: "Amen. Miracle. Miracle. Amen."

Eugenia's and *Valeria's* Song

They did not go to the wild places,
but you will go.

I will go with tobacco and corn.
I will go with the harvest of my garden.
I will go with empty hands
and a song of gratitude in my voice.

They did not go to the wilderness,
but you will go.

I will go . . . and the leaves
will tremble their welcome song.
The birds will be silent to hear me . . .
and then they will join me in song.

They did not go to the forest,
but you will go.

I will go often and the sky will open
like a great bonfire
of calls and responses:
stories, songs,
dances, drums.

They did not go to the wild places,
but you will go.

I will go. Many of us will go.
The bright, shining eyes of all of our ancestors
will light our way.
The moon through the forest ceiling will guide us.
And all of our people who love our land . . .
we will know what to do.

They did not go to the forest,
but you will go.

I will. *Aché.* I will go.
I will. *Aché.* I will go.
Amen, *Jan Jan Katú.*
Amen. *Ajó.* Amen.

Glossary

Glossary

•

abuela, abuelo: elder, ancestor; literally, grandmother, grandfather.

aché: blessings or divine grace in Lucumí, an Afro-caribbean religion of Yoruba origin.

ajó: amen of the Lakota people of North America. This amen is used today by many indigenous-identified boricuas during healing ceremonies.

algarroba: fruit of the tropical carob tree *(Hymenaea courbaril)*. Algarroba is an important supplemental source of protein, B vitamins, iron and calcium. Once disparaged for its complex aroma, *algarroba* is now being sold as a high-end super food over the internet. The algarroba tree's medicinal resin and attractive hard wood have made this tree one of the region's most valuable resources through the centuries.

Almácigo: neighborhood named after the native *almácigo* tree *(Bursera simaruba)*, associated with the survival of our people since pre-Columbian times. The broth —made from its sustainably-harvested, resinous bark with local salt and medicinal condiments— is rich in minerals and micronutrients rare in foods cultivated in superficial soils. During famine, energizing *almácigo* broths sustained our people by combating anemia. The resin of this tree also has fungicidal, antiseptic, pectoral, diuretic and stomach-healing properties. Smudges made by burning almácigo resin accompany prayers, figure in ceremonies of spiritual purification and repel mosquitos and other insects. Because of its high concentration of flammable resin, pieces of *almácigo* wood were kept smoldering in kitchen hearths *(fogones)* in order to quickly light the firewood or charcoal used for cooking.

Atabey, Atabeira: mother goddess of the Taíno culture, often depicted squatting to give birth. Our cover illustration depicts an Afro-Taína Atabey dressed as the Catholic Mother of Miracles. A syncretism of our three basic cultures, she is a Boricua divinity proposed by the author and cover illustrator Saraivy Orench Reinat.

¡Ay bendito!: exclamation roughly translatable as "oh dear" or "poor thing." This empathetic phrase is very identified with the character of the Puerto Rican people who traditionally respond to the difficult situations of others with great generosity.

babalao: priest of Lucumí, an Afro-caribbean religion of Yoruba origin. As earthly representatives of Orula, *babalaos* practice the ancient oracular system of Ifá. This oracle includes throwing specially prepared pieces of coconut shell and interpreting the results as a means to find the cause of any given situation as well as the best ways to reestablish balance.

barefoot doctors: traditional healers educated by gifted elders, often too "poor" to wear shoes.

barriada: a sub-*barrio*, usually a street or two with a specific personality, and often one sole entrance/exit.

barrio: neighborhood, community.

batey: a cleared space used for socializing, domestic work and ceremonies, often located in backyards and community centers. Traditionally, *bateyes* are created by clearing an area and then pummeling the earth until it is rock-hard and easy to sweep clean. On their outer borders, *bateyes* are often planted with medicinal and culinary plants, including useful trees.

Blanca, lady Blanca, doña Blanca: cocaine.

boliche: the uppermost tobacco leaves of inferior quality.

la bolita: an illegal, 3-digit, national numbers game.

bolitero: local organizer of la *bolita*, often seen as a type of down-home banker.

bomba: musical form developed by Afro-Rican populations, mostly associated with life on our sugarcane plantations. To this day, *bomba* drums are called *barriles* or barrels, since drummers first used repaired barrels used for the rum distilled on these plantations. La *bomba's* diverse rhythms *(leró, cuembé, yubá, gracimá, holandés, sicá, etc.)* originate in the cultures of the Africans who were enslaved in Puerto Rico. *Bomba* is typically played with two or three barrel-shaped drums, one of which responds to the song lyrics and the movements of solo dancers. One singer plays a large maraca while the *cuá* stick marks counterpoint rhythms on the side of a drum.

bombazo: bomba party.

boricua: Puerto Rican. (Puerto Rico's indigenous name is Borikén; thus her people are *boricuas.*)

Borinquen, Boriquén, Borikén, Boriké, Burenken:
transcriptions of the original, Taíno name for Puerto Rico's
main island.

brujo: shaman, botanical healer, traditional natural healer,
witch.

buenas noches: good night.

burén: original cooking surface from pre-Colombian times: a
pan made of clay or metal used to toast grains and prepare
casabe and other traditional dishes.

café con leche: coffee with milk.

calalú: afro-Caribbean soup made from lots of nutritious
wild leaves, especially blero *(Amaranthus spp.)* but also
purslane *(Portulaca oleracea)*, friendly Caribbean nettle
(Laportea aestuans), Spanish needles *(Bidens spp.)*, black
nightshade *(Solanum americanum)*, etc.

cañón: pistol, in street slang.

¡Carájila!: a strong (for a woman of her time) exclamation of
displeasure.

¡Caramba!: a common exclamation of surprise or dismay.

casabe: our indigenous "bread", made from finely-grated
cassava or manioc, salt and perhaps other ingredients. A
good survival food that can be stored for long periods of
time without spoiling.

cemí: a triangular sculpture sacred to the Tainos. Sculpted
in stone, wood or other materials, and adorned with
important symbols, traditional *cemíes* represented the

physical essence of the deities. Some *cemíes* seem to represent the feminine aspect of creation (fertile earth), which rises up to meet the sky. On the cover of this book, our Afro-Taína Mother of Miracles rises from a cemí.

charco: here, a natural pool in a body of running water.

Charco Prieto: literally, black pool. Here, the name of a swimming hole.

cigar factory: During the 19th and the beginning of the 20th centuries, Puerto Rico's cigar factories were the peoples' universities. In the silence of their craft, cigar makers elected readers, who were sometimes paid by the workers themselves, to read to them the world news, novels, philosophical texts, *The Bible* and other literary works. Debates and other intellectual exchanges were part of the culture of this workplace.

colmado: small, neighborhood supermarket or grocery store.

cokaine: cocaine; intentionally spelled with k to distance the synthesized alkaloid from the greatly medicinal coca plant *(Erythroxylon coca)*.

compañero: companion; here, a sentimental partner; common-law husband.

coquí: generic name for all Puerto Rican singing tree frogs *(Eleutherodactylus spp., etc.)*, which hatch from their eggs as tiny frogs, eliminating the tadpole phase. *Coquíes*, named onomatopoeically to imitate the males' loud mating call, are a symbol of the beloved natural world of Borikén. Since some species can only survive on Puerto Rico's islands, the coquí has also come to symbolize our people's national identity and deep connection to the archipelago.

¡coño carajo!: a strong expression of frustration and anger.

corazón *(Annona reticulate)*: Antillean fruit in the form of an anatomical heart, with an aromatic, creamy, white pulp. The corazón tree's leaves are used medicinally to strengthen the human heart and to treat indigestion and colitis. The seeds are used to make very effective insecticides for head lice, fleas and agricultural pests.

corona: literally crown. Here, the leaves close to the top of the tobacco plant.

culantro; also **recao** *(Eryngium foetidum)*: a wild and cultivated seasoning plant basic to Puerto Rican cuisine. *Culantro* smells and tastes somewhat like cilantro, and has important medicinal uses as a digestive aid and blood pressure remedy also used to treat menstrual cramps and malaria.

curandera/o: traditional healer recognized for her or his nature-centered wisdom. Some *curanderas* specialize in botanical medicine; others in setting bones or other types of physical or emotional therapy. Some are shamans, specializing in spiritual integration. A new generation of curanderos integrates formal education with traditional wisdom.

dolores, Dolores: literally sorrows or suffering. María Dolores is a common name in Spanish for women named after Our Lady of Sorrows. Lola is a common nickname for María Dolores. In the title, this word has a double meaning, since it corresponds to the protagonist (Lola) as well as to the sorrows described throughout the text.

don, doña: title of warm respect, usually used for older men and women, respectively.

doña Blanca: cocaine.

dos: two.

el inocente: the innocent one.

El Vocero: somewhat sensationalist newspaper.

empacho: a digestive illness characterized by abdominal swelling, constipation and pain, once common among Puerto Rican children. Traditionally, *empachos* are cured with special prayers, abdominal massage and digestive or purgative teas.

escoba, escobilla (Sida spp.): wild, wiry antiseptic herbs used to wash dishes, bathe animals, make brooms, disinfect wounds, staunch bleeding and more.

espiritista: member of a spiritual community that communicates directly with the deceased in order to receive guidance, "find out what really happened," and facilitate healings, exorcisms, etc.

exacto: straight, without variation (for the biggest prize).

fogón: traditional rustic, outdoor kitchen fueled by firewood or homemade charcoal.

fonda: a small cafeteria or home-based lunch place.

galletas María: round, semi-sweet cookies wrapped in paper rolls and traditionally enjoyed with *café* con *leche*, hot chocolate, etc.

gandules *(Cajanus cajan)*: pigeon peas. Of African origin, gandules are Puerto Rico's national legume. Gandules (known to combat sickle cell anemia) are the principal ingredient of many traditional dishes, and an important source of protein and iron.

guábaras *(Atya spp.)*: various small, fresh-water prawn species. These clawless, filter feeders may measure up to 5" long.

guamá: the thin-pulped, semi-sweet fruits of *Inga quarternata* or *Inga fagifolia* trees. These legume species help to fertilize our forests, and are especially common in coffee and cacao plantations.

guanábana: a green-colored fruit known in the English speaking Caribbean as soursop. The *guanabana* is covered with soft spines and is full of delicious, sub-acid white pulp and lots of black seeds. Fruit of the *guanábano*.

guanábano *(Annona muricata)*: tropical tree, source of *guanábana* or soursop fruits. Its aromatic leaves are used in remedies for stomach upsets, intestinal gas, high blood pressure, cancer and other conditions.

guanimes de maíz con coco: Puerto Rican tamales made from corn meal and salt; sometimes moistened with coconut milk and seasoned with brown sugar and fennel or anise seeds.

guaraguao *(Guarea guidonia)*: common native tree of the mahogany family with reddish wood and a distinctive patina. Much used for traditional stringed instruments, barrels and other recipients for wines and rum. Its astringent leaves are used in medicine. The name *guaraguao* also refers to Puerto Rico's red-tailed hawk *(Buteo jamaicensis)*.

guayacán *(Guaiacum officinale)*: Puerto Rico's most valuable, slow-growing, long-living, super-dense hardwood tree, with an array of medicinal properties and industrial uses.

guayabo *(Psidium guajava)*: small tree famous throughout the tropics for its medicinal leaves and its delicious guava fruit, used to make juices and sweets. The guayabo's hard wood is especially coveted for cooking, both as firewood and as charcoal, as it burns slowly, evenly and long. Here, a most formidable weapon.

Hacienda La Torre: literally, The Tower Plantation. In barrio Piñales, the name of a nearby sugar cane plantation.

hidionda *(Cassia occidentalis, Senna occidentalis)*: an Antillean, leguminous weed with seeds that can be roasted, ground and boiled to make a coffee-like drink with a chocolatey taste. The leaves, roots and flowers of this plant are used in several traditional medicinal formulas for post-childbirth conditions, intestinal gas and liver complaints.

Ifá: orisha of the sacred oracle.

independentista: person identified with the ideal of political and economic sovereignty for Puerto Rico.

el inocente: the innocent one.

jabón azul: blue soap; a traditional, indigo-tinted soap, especially valued for washing clothes by hand.

jan jan katú: amen of the Taínos, indigenous people of Burenken (Puerto Rico).

jíbaro: the resourceful, knowledgeable, independent agricultural people of Puerto Rico. Also, in popular usage, a "country bumpkin" who has yet to learn the street-wise ways of urban life.

Jurakán: Taíno divinity of storms. This Taíno word is the root for the word hurricane in several languages.

la bolita: an illegal, 3-digit, national numbers game.

lerén (Calathea allouia): sweet-corn root; a small, crunchy, starchy root vegetable *(vianda)* native to the Caribbean.

madre, Madre: mother, Mother.

maguey (Agave gigantea, Furcraea gigantea): native agave plant used as a source of fiber for sacks, fishing lines, ropes, hammocks and more. Its roots are used as a stimulating blood purifier, and are prized for curing native rums. Its pulp, which must be softened over a fire, is an important source of medicine for the lungs and bronchial passages.

Mai, Mami: Mommy; pronounced like my and mommy, respectively.

malagueta *(Pimenta racemosa)*: bay rum; an Antillean native of the eucalyptus family with antiseptic, antiviral, anti-inflammatory and analgesic properties. Especially prized for liniments and baths.

malanga *(Colocasia spp.)*: dasheen, taro root; a starchy root vegetable *(vianda)* grown in moist terrain, native to the Asian tropics.

mamey *(Mammea americana)*: an Antillean tree that bears a large, round fruit with delicious, hard, orange flesh tasting something like a peach. All parts of this tree repel or kill mosquitos, and an important insecticide is derived from its seeds.

manos a la obra: all hands to work. This was the phrase used by Puerto Rico's ex-governor Luis Muñoz Marín to motivate the people to participate in the industrial boom during the 1950's'. This boom, fueled by big subsidies and tax breaks for U.S. corporations on the island, contributed to the demise of Puerto Rico's agricultural traditions.

maya *(Bromelia penguin)*: a spiny plant similar to, but much larger than, a pineapple, used as a green, living fence.

Mayagüez, mayagüezano: university town on Puerto Rico's west coast; native of Mayagüez.

menjunje: any complex home remedy.

mi hija: my daughter; a term of intergenerational affection that is most often not taken literally. **mi hijo:** my son.

mi reina: my queen.

milagros: miracles. **María de los Milagros** (named after the Virgin known as the Blessed Mother of Miracles) is a common name for women, who go by Milagros, Millie and other nicknames. In the title of this book, *milagros* has a double meaning, since the name of our protagonist is Manuel Milagros, and the theme of miracles is central to this work.

Milagrosa: literally, miraculous or miracle worker. Here, the Mother of Miracles, sometimes known as the Virgen, is an important manifestation of the Divine Mother.

Murió Amelia. Amelia, ¿qué pasó? Murió Ameleia, se fue y me dejó: Amelia died. Amelia, what happened? Amelia died. She went and left me, oh!

ñame (Dioscorea spp. etc.): starchy, root vegetables, mostly of African origin, with a prodigious ability to sprout and grow even in the shade of our subtropical forests.

newyorican: a Puerto Rican raised in New York or (often) any another place in the U.S.A.

nuestra gente: our people.

números bonitos, números feos: literally pretty numbers, ugly numbers.

oranges: here, this word refers to the sour oranges used to wash and marinate fresh goat meat. This marinade enhances taste and helps to tenderize the meat.

orisha: divinity of the ancient Afro-caribbean Yoruba or Lucumí religion, sometimes known as *Santería.* Each *orisha* represents an element or force of nature. During slavery, practicing the ancient African religions was a crime punishable by death. Enslaved populations were forced to worship Catholic saints. As a result, throughout the Caribbean, the *orishas* have been identified (syncretized) with European saints, according to the symbolism associated with each saint. For example, Changó, orisha of thunder and lightning (as well as drums), is identified with Saint Barbara, who is always depicted standing next to a lightning bolt. This syncretism permitted the enslaved population to practice their own religion without arousing the suspicion of their "owners."

oronés *(Polygala paniculata)*: diminutive herb with white flowers. Its roots smell distinctly of wintergreen and, like wintergreen leaves, are a source of salicylic acid, aspirin in its natural form.

oye: Hey! Literally, "Listen!"

Pai, Papi: pop, dad; pronounced like (apple) pie and poppy, respectively.

palma Christi *(Ricinus comunis)*: castor bean plant. This bush's ability to alleviate pain and inflammation has earned it the Latin folk name as the "hand of Christ" *(palma Christi)*. Its poisonous seeds are the source of castor oil, used externally to fight viral skin conditions and reduce inflammation. Internally, this same oil is taken as a laxative. Castor oil *(aceite de higuereta, aceite de ricino)* was once produced domestically around the island.

Peluquería Los Remedios: Los Remedios Beauty Salón. Los Remedios is a Sevillian neighborhood named for the Virgin of Remedies. Its double meaning implies that this salon offers remedies for the esthetically challenged!

perico: cocaine. *Perico* is literally a parakeet or parrot, associated with surprising verbal abilities. Cocaine is a stimulant that gives partakers the gift of gab.

pilón: traditionally, a wooden mortar used with its pestle *(maceta)* daily to mash up seasoning herbs such as garlic, oregano, hot pepper, etc.

pinpín: cocaine.

Piñales: a place where pineapples are cultivated; in this case, the name of this *barrio* serves as a historical reminder that pineapples were once grown there.

poleo *(Lippia alba* var. *Puerto Rico)*: native, aromatic bush; its leaves and flowers are used for an endless array of remedies for cough, colds, digestive woes, and to ease menstrual cramps.

pomarrosa *(Syzygium jambos)*: rose apple, a delicate, round, cream colored fruit that (somewhat like its red, pear-shaped relative *Syzygium malaccense*) smells and tastes of roses. Here, it is the portal from the forest (Osaín's territory) to the river (Oshun's territory). Oshun's preferred offerings include copper and gold colored metals, fruits and flowers).

que te aproveche, buen provecho: typical blessings conferred upon people who are eating. Literally, "may your food be good for you!"

recao, also **culantro** *(Eryngium foetidum):* a wild (and cultivated) seasoning plant basic to Puerto Rican cuisine.

Recao smells and tastes somewhat like cilantro, and has important medicinal uses as a digestive aid and blood pressure remedy also used to treat menstrual cramps and malaria.

rociados de yuca: semi-sweet, traditional, gourmet dish, still available in Loíza. Cooked and served wrapped in banana leaves, *rociados* are made with cassava *(yuca),* coconut, fennel seeds and other seasonal ingredients. The recipe for *rociados* can be found in *El Burén de Lula,* a beautiful Loíza-style cookbook by María Dolores de Jesús.

rompezaragüey, santa maría (Eupatorium odoratum): a vigorous, aromatic herb used throughout the Antilles to liberate or purify people of negative energies associated with manipulation and malice.

ruda (Ruta chalepensis): an herbaceous plant with small, bluish leaves, highly prized as an analgesic and anti-inflammatory. It contains salicylic acid, a natural form of aspirin.

salsagorda (salsa gorda): salsa of the 1960's and '70's, characterized by emphasis on Afro-Caribbean percussion and street-style voices.

sancocho: traditional stew made of starchy root vegetables *(viandas),* meat, local wild greens and condiments.

santa maría de playa (Lantana involucrata): native, aromatic bush used in baths for fever and several viral conditions.

santero: member of the ancient Afro-Caribbean Yoruba or Lucumí religion, sometimes known as *Santería.* The *orishas* (divinities) of this religion personify the elements and forces of nature. Participants use specific rhythms, songs, dances and sacrifices of fruits, flowers, and animals in order to communicate directly with the *orishas.*

Taíno: the peace-loving, agricultural/fishing and foraging people of Arawak origin who inhabited Borikén for centuries before and at the time of the Spanish invasion. In spite of their documented historical "extinction," recent studies of matrilineal DNA as well as linguistic, culinary, medicinal and other Puerto Rican traditions prove a lasting Taíno presence throughout our archipelago.

tapas: in Spain, snacks offered on small plates, traditionally enjoyed with wine or beer.

tembleque de coco: a traditional, sweet, cinnamon-topped coconut pudding that shakes *(tiembla)* something like gelatin. Thus, its name, *tembleque.*

tijerilla *(Fregata magnificens)*: frigate bird, scissor tail; large sea bird most often seen flying over coastal waters.

tijerillas en tierra, tormenta en la mar: Puerto Rican saying; literally "frigate birds on land, hurricane at sea."

tormenta: hurricane, big storm.

tortilla de yuca: traditional, gourmet Afro-Rican dish made with cassava *(yuca),* coconut milk, brown sugar and spices. Today, this is a rare, slow-food specialty featured in *El Burén de Lula,* a beautiful Loíza-style cook book by María Dolores de Jesús.

trece pesos exacto: thirteen dollars straight.

vetiver *(Vetiveria zizanioides)*: an aromatic grass known as *pacholí* in Puerto Rico. Its earthy-smelling aromatic roots and the essential oil expressed from them are used as a calming anti-depressant, deodorant, insect repellent and more. Essential oil of vetiver has been used for centuries as a fixative in the perfume industry.

viandas: the starchy vegetables that are the pillars of the Puerto Rican diet. Among others: cassava, taro, breadfruit, plantains, sweet potatoes, yams, pumpkin, etc.

El Vocero: somewhat sensationalist newspaper.

yaguas: the thick, fibrous sheaths that surround the upper, green part of our native royal palm. *Yaguas* fold into triangular cylinders of useful, durable fiber used to build rustic walls, carry objects, wash clothing, and much more.

yarey *(Sabal spp.)*: an Antillean palm with a thick trunk and enormous, fan-shaped leaves. From pre-Colombian times, *yarey* leaves have been woven to make roofs and walls, hats, baskets, mats and even hammocks.

yautía *(Xanthosoma spp.)*: tanier root, a flavorful, starchy root vegetable *(vianda)* native to our Central American region.

yo: I, me.

yuca *(Manihot esculenta)*: cassava, manioc; source of tapioca. This was the principal root vegetable of Puerto Rico's native Taíno Indians.

Verses discovered in barrio Almácigo
early in the 20th century

O Milagrosa, abuela Diosa:
Vida, Justicia y Sanación.
Creastes tierra, luna y estrellas.
¡Amor infinito, Madre de Dios!

Oh, Grandmother Goddess of Miracles:
Life, Justice, Healing, All.
Creator of stars, the moon and our Earth.
You are infinite love, Oh, Mother of God.

•

La divina Madre de virgen la vistieron.
Esconder su gran poder los grandes quisieron.

They dressed as a virgin the Great Mother Divine.
Let's hide her power, was the big shots' plan.

•

Su divino hijo tan pobre que nació.
Lo del mundo terrenal es todo el opuesto.
Lo grande es chico; lo pobre es rico;
La virgen inocente, Madre del Gran Misterio.

Her divine son was born so poor.
All is the opposite in this world.
The penniless are true; the big wigs, truly small;
An innocent virgin is Mother of All.